BLURB

In a world full of monsters, I'm the insane one.

A simmering rage lies just beneath the surface, one that can't be controlled.

The voice in my head protects me, unleashing quick death, unhinged brutality.

One fateful night three years ago, I became the judge, jury, and executioner.

Losing my freedom when all I wanted was to escape.

Now, I'm locked away.

Imprisoned in a hell so torturous, my nightmares have become a reprieve.

Nothing could've prepared me for my doctor. My tormentor.

Dr. Atlas Stone.

He says all the right things, the one person who truly understands me. I gave him what little trust I had left.

The sadist who causes me more pain than I could've fathomed. The unpredictable psychopath who thrives on controlling my mind, and my body.

I've become nothing more than a pawn in his wicked game of obsession and experimentation.

Welcome to Wellard Asylum.

Where the darkness swallows you whole and frees your inner monster.

PROLOGUE
OLIVIA

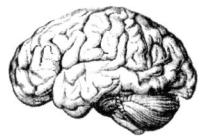

"Your son has fucking raped me for months!" I scream at the top of my lungs, my hate and disgust igniting the fuse connected to the ticking time bomb inside my head.

"You've corrupted my baby with your whore ways!" My stepmother seethes, and I laugh hysterically, wondering what fucking universe she lives in.

This bitch is delusional, and I feel my control unraveling. "He took my virginity, you psycho cunt! He held me down, ripped my clothes off, and violated my body against my fucking will."

"Lies!" She screeches, the high-pitched sound snapping the invisible link tethering logic to my sanity.

White hot rage simmers beneath my skin, a pulsing sensation taking root in the center of my forehead. My chest tightens uncomfortably, heat flushing my entire upper body.

She knows I have anger issues, yet she continues to push me. I've told her repeatedly to back the fuck off, I can't control my emotions once they hit their peak.

Does she listen? *No.*

She won't stop defending her demon spawn long enough to heed the warning signs.

"I'll say this one last time," I grit out. "Keep your fucking son away from me."

He stole my innocence while I fought him tooth and nail. Swinging my fists, kicking my legs, sinking my teeth into any part of his body I could reach.

It did nothing.

He slammed his fist into the side of my head, knocking me out cold. I came to as he sprayed my chest with his cum, saying over and over how beautiful my blood looked on his cock. He left shortly after, and I spent an hour in the shower, alternating between puking my guts up, and scrubbing my skin raw.

She knows the truth, but she'll deny it until the day she dies. Which may be tonight if she doesn't walk away *now.*

"You little bitch!" She screams, backhanding me across the face.

My head whips to the side, momentarily stunned until my eyes land on the fire poker sitting in the rack. The pulsing in my forehead quickly morphs into piercing, throbbing pain, engulfing my entire skull as it roars to life. My vision dims at the corners of my eyes, sweat beading above my brows.

"Do it!" A voice penetrates through the ringing in my ears, a sudden wave of calm taking over. *"Do it!"*

My hand shoots out, wrapping my fingers around the iron poker, a sense of rightness blanketing me as I pull it from the black, metal stand. Spinning around, shock registers on my stepmother's face as I plunge it into her abdomen, the hook of the poker disappearing inside her belly. Tearing through tissue and muscles, I don't stop pushing until I hear the popping of her skin, the rod protruding from her back. A putrid smell permeates the air in the room but I don't acknowledge the waste spilling from her intestines, poisoning her body as I watch her face contort in anguish, her suffering bringing me satisfaction.

She screams in agony, and I smile, meeting resistance as I attempt to pull the poker from her stomach. The iron tip reappears after some effort, her intestines dangling from the hook.

I feel like I've gone fishing.

My father bellows from the other side of the living room as she falls to her knees, her usually tan skin ghostly pale. She gasps for air as he runs to her side, falling to his knees, screaming her name. "Linda! Linda!"

"Shut the fuck up, Dad!" I cackle, jerking the poker back and forth until her insides plop on the floor beside him, the sickly moist sound almost as atrocious as the foul odor depletes the oxygen from the room.

My father turns his head, locking his gaze on me, pure hatred in his eyes.

He stayed in the kitchen this entire time, allowing his new wife to scream and assault his own flesh and blood. His only child. He didn't say a word or come to my defense. I don't know why I expected more from the man who raised me. There was a time in my life when I looked up to him. He was caring, helpful, and present. Since meeting the cunt currently bleeding out on the floor, he's become angry, resentful, and quick to knock me to the ground.

I knew I didn't matter anymore the day he announced their engagement. I begged him not to marry her, told him what Scott was doing to me. As soon as the words left my mouth, he backhanded me, demanding I stop making up stories just because I don't like them. That was the day I realized I was on my own, abandoned by the man meant to protect me. I vowed to myself as soon as I turn eighteen, I'd leave this hell hole.

He rises to his feet, taking a menacing step towards me. My fingers tighten around the poker, readying myself to kill the man who helped create me.

"You little bitch," he grits out, taking another step forward.

"Come any closer, and you'll be dead before you hit the floor."

"I made your mother leave when she beat the shit out of you. I should've let her fucking kill you."

His words should sting, but I feel nothing.

My biological mother was an addict. He didn't make her leave because she was physically abusing me. He got rid of her because she was draining him financially, and we never heard from her again. The loving father I knew as a little girl is gone, replaced by the pathetic man standing in front of me now. He chose his new family over me.

He didn't protect me from the monster in the room across from mine. He knew, and did absolutely nothing to stop it. "And I wish she would've fucked anyone other than you, but here we are, old man." I grin, noticing Linda's chest has stopped moving in my peripheral vision.

His face darkens to a crimson as if his head is about to blow off his shoulders. His fists clench at his sides, his stance widening, readying himself for a fight.

Please. Fucking. Do. It.

My wish is granted when he lunges forward, both his hands flying to my throat. My reflexes are catlike as I jump back, raising the fire poker with lightning speed, swinging it like a batter going for the season's record home run. It connects with his temple, the hook sinking into his skull with a squelch. He falls to the floor with a thud, into a heap beside his beloved, dead wife.

Blood gushes from his head, seeping into the rug beneath him. I watch with fascination as the crimson liquid stains the cream material, the area growing larger until it meets Linda's.

He rocks from side to side, cradling his head, whimpering. "Please. I'm your father," he whines, pleading for mercy.

Moving to stand over him, I plant my feet on either side of his neck. "You're nothing to me." Positioning the poker at his throat, I slam it into his jugular, blood spraying my lower body and the floor around us.

His hands fly to his throat, gasping for the oxygen just out of reach. Pulling the poker from his neck, my skin prickles as I watch him suffer, the adrenaline in my veins pumping harder than ever before.

His eyes widen comically before slowly drooping as his breaths become shallow, slower, a satisfying death rattle vibrating his chest. Wetness blooms between his legs, the smell of his urine mixing with the smell of her shit.

A hysterical laugh bubbles up my throat, and I fall to my knees beside his dying body, bending down to whisper into his ear. "Rot in hell, cunt." His chest deflates for the final time, and I fall back onto my ass.

Fuck, that felt good.

My body trembles, the urge to kill still in the forefront of my mind. I struggle to calm my racing heart, my fingers tapping away on my knees. I have to stop this. I need to get out of here.

"There's one left!" The voice in my head argues, and I begin counting to snap myself out of this murderous prison.

One.

Two.

Three.

Four.

With every number I speak, my fingers connect with the skin over my kneecap. My mind is spiraling, and I continue counting until my body stops trembling all together.

I've never reached this level of insanity before, the counting usually bringing me back before things get out of hand. It's only happened a few times before, at school, always triggered by some little cunt running her mouth. Dad was pissed when I put the last girl in the hospital, the bruises from the beating marring my skin for two weeks. He punished me for something I can't control, something I hardly remembered. It was like a switch flipped, and I was a different person.

Sometimes it feels like there's another being living inside me. I'm in a constant battle with the stranger in my head, and when it comes to my emotions being heightened, it always wins.

Glancing at the two dead bodies beside me, reality sets in along with the gravity of what I've done. My chest tightens, terrified of the consequences of my actions. Just as the panic threatens to cripple me, the voice returns. *"I've got you."*

My body relaxes, a floating sensation making the air around me lighter, more comforting. The smells disappear along with any guilt or worry I felt only a few moments ago.

Two less assholes in the world.

One more to go.

The front door creaks open, snapping me back to my present situation. When I look up, my eyes clash with my tormentor, my stepbrother. His jaw drops as he takes in the scene, his gaze lingering on his mother for a few short moments. He steps further into the room, my skin buzzing with awareness.

Danger.

He's only seventeen, but his large, imposing form and evil demeanor has me second guessing my ability to overpower him. I'm strong as hell when my anger takes over, but he could easily subdue me without much effort.

My mind reels as I glance around, waiting for an idea to hit me. I silently curse the voice in my head for making the decision to kill Scott but offering no help in doing so. All thoughts disappear as he comes to stand in front of me, offering his hand. Quickly masking my surprise, I slide my fingers across his palm, and he pulls me up, wrapping his arms around me.

"What happened, little sister?" He whispers against my cheek, my stomach roiling at his closeness.

His warm breath whisps across my face, a single throb in my head signaling what's coming. I'm fighting my own mind to stay in control so I can carry out my plan to kill this motherfucker.

"Your mom slapped me," I whisper, playing the obedient little stepsister he's come to know.

I fought like hell the first time he sexually assaulted me, but after he knocked me out, being complicit and conscious seemed smarter. I wanted to know what was happening to me. Up to this point, I've disassociated during the act, planning my getaway once I'm alone. My eighteenth birthday is only a couple of months away. All I had to do was wait, but my temper fucked everything up.

No. That bitch fucked it up, and now I have to improvise.

"She got what she deserved for touching you." He grins, pulling me into his chest.

That's rich coming from you.

Bile rises in my throat as his warm touch seeps into my skin. "You're not mad?" I ask innocently.

Keep the chunks down, Olivia.

He leans back, tilting my chin to meet his gaze. "Of course not, sweetheart. We'll get you cleaned up, toss the place, and call the police. They'll think it was a break in."

"Okay." I agree, squeezing my eyes closed to ease the throbbing against my skull. This war with myself is exhausting. I'm so fucking tired from the back and forth within my mind. I just want to be normal.

He leads me into the bathroom, stripping off my clothes, his hungry gaze roaming every inch of my body. I let him look his fill, fighting the urge to reach for my toothbrush, and shove it through his eye socket. After removing his own clothes, he turns on the spray, leading me into the shower once the water is warm. "It's okay. I'm going to take care of you."

My mind screams to rip the shower head off the wall, and use it to cave in his skull but I dismiss the idea.

For now.

Staring at the floor as he scrubs my body, I hyperfocus on the bloody water trailing down my legs, circling the drain. My vision dims once more as he pushes the cloth between my legs, sweeping back and forth, applying pressure against my core.

"Hold on! Not yet!" I scream internally as my body begins to tremble.

He reaches around, sliding the cloth between my ass cheeks and my jaw clenches, my skin burning like molten lava.

"Do it!" The voice screams, and I'm powerless against the explosion behind my eyes, the loss of control over my body. It's as if I'm watching from the sidelines as I become the apex predator, my sights locked on the weak, pathetic prey.

Raising my hand to his cheek, he mistakes the move as an affectionate gesture. My palm slides to the center of his face, and I shove him hard, pure hate and adrenaline fueling what happens next.

The back of his head crashes into the glass door of the shower, the frosted pane shattering from the impact. He bellows, cursing as he reaches for me, and I plaster myself against the wall, gripping the metal bar tightly. Time slows, his arms flailing wildly, desperately searching for anything to grab onto as he falls through the frame, crashing onto the tile floor.

My shoulders shake with laughter at the sight of blood trickling from his body, filling the grout lines beneath him. Tiny shards of glass penetrate the majority of his skin, resembling a human pin cushion. He screams my name, pleading for help through his tears, but the focal point of my attention is a piece of glass lying next to the toilet. It's size and shape remind me of a slice of pizza, and I know exactly what I want to do with it.

Stepping out of the shower, I bend down and pick it up, the sharp edge nicking my palm. Crimson seeps from the cut, but I don't feel any pain. Slowly, I squat down beside him, my gaze running the length of his form, halting where his flaccid cock lies against his thigh. My uninjured hand slides down his abdomen, over his pelvis, circling his length firmly with my fingers. He shouts obscenities, attempting to get up, but every time he moves, it drives the glass deeper inside his skin, blood gushing from the wounds where the larger pieces are embedded. It's not until his gaze clashes with mine; he falls silent.

He takes notice.

I'm no longer myself. I'm simply a vessel filled with hate and fury. I'm the abused, little stepsister about to take his life.

Blood trickles down my arm as I lift the glass to his cock, jaggedly sawing through the weapon he's abused me with for months. His lifeforce sprays from the appendage, coating me in slickness. His mouth is moving, but the ringing in my ears prevents me from hearing whatever he's saying.

As I slice through the last shred of skin connecting his cock to his body, the bleeding slows to a thick stream, oozing down his thighs, staining the bright, white tile. Lifting his dick in my hand, our blood mingles, our bodily fluids merging together for the last time.

I bet he's not turned on now.

His face pales and his body trembles as I hover over him, tracking the tears leaking from his eyes. His suffering brings me peace, and I feel nothing as he silently pleads for this torment to end.

Lifting my hand, I hold his cock in front of his face as if in offering. He whimpers, and I realize my intimidating abuser is nothing more than a terrified child. Gripping his jaw, I force his mouth open, shoving his limp cock between his lips. Using my fingertips, I press it as far as I can, ensuring it fills every inch of space in his throat. "Our blood looks so beautiful on your cock, big brother." I giggle, throwing his words back at him from the night he stole my virginity.

He gags, trying to dislodge the mangled organ from his throat, but I cover his mouth with my hand, holding it in place. His hands fly up, his fists delivering weakened blows to my chest. He struggles as I hold my position, unwilling to give him the tiniest sliver of mercy. He's choking, and every time his body jerks, tears leak from his eyes, a burst of blood shooting from the wound where his cock used to be. His body begins convulsing, and I roll my eyes, patiently waiting for him to fucking die already.

This goes on for what seems like forever, but finally, his body goes slack, his eyes rolling back in his head. Removing my hand from his mouth, I'm met with stillness and silence as I check his pulse.

He's dead.

They say when you enter hell, you relive the worst moment of your life every single day. The thought brings a smile to my face, knowing he'll live in this moment forever, always seeing me, unable to touch me.

My knees ache as I stand up after being in a squatting position for so long. I wait for the feeling to return to my legs, the pins and needles sensation making me chuckle and curse. Stepping over his body, I leave the bathroom naked, covered in blood. As I enter my bedroom, the sound of sirens in the distance has me halting.

I guess the neighbors heard the screams.

I make my way over to my bed, sitting on the edge, tapping my fingers against my knees as the sirens get closer. My heart rate slows, and I breathe deeply as my mind becomes my own again. Two words replay in my head over and over.

I'm fucked. I'm fucked.

Anxiety slams into me, and I begin counting the letters of the words I'm reciting, including the apostrophe and the period. It equals an even number. *Ten.* A deep breath of relief leaves my chest, and I feel a little better.

Standing from the bed, I slide on a t-shirt and shorts, heading for the living room. As I pass through the doorway, I flip the light switch off and on four times. Closing the door behind me, I'm sure to push on it four times, ensuring it's latched before continuing down the hall. I count each footfall as I gaze at my feet, coming to stop at the edge of the room on the sixteenth step.

The front door crashes open, police entering the house with guns drawn, trained on me. "Get down on the floor!" They all scream, and I drop to the floor, lying on my stomach, hands above my head.

I'm so fucked.

Everything will be okay. I still have my even number. *Twelve.*

CHAPTER ONE
OLIVIA

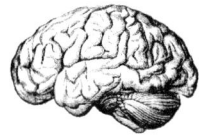

My nose is itching like a motherfucker, but I can't scratch it strapped to a gurney.

I've lost all feeling in my hands, and my forehead aches from the pressure of the leather strap holding my head in place. The flickering fluorescent lights swaying from the ceiling are painfully blinding, my eyes sensitive from all the medications they've pumped into my body. The old metal gurney makes for a bumpy ride, and the only sound I hear is the whining of the wheels against the concrete floor.

Maddening.

I assumed I was making progress with my treatment, Dr. Sweeney fueling my delusions, praising my hard work and cooperation. I thought I was on a healthy road to rehabilitation, but the joke's on me.

It was all a lie.

He didn't give a fuck about me, steadily counting the days to his retirement, not the least bit concerned about my wellbeing. I began feeling safe, slowly letting my guard down around him, accepting his help like the good little patient I was. I kept to myself, never causing any trouble, but in the end, it was all for nothing. He retired, and I've been transferred to another facility.

Wellard Asylum.

Home to the criminally insane and depraved. I've heard people whisper about this place, and now that I'm here, I get it.

Two male nurses roll me down the creepy hallway, the smell of piss and shit assaulting my nostrils. A sense of dread overcomes me, the energy in this place feels oppressive and lifeless. My senses pick up on it just from my view of the ceiling, and I'm not sure I want to see the rest of it.

The obnoxious lights dim as I'm rolled into a room, my eyes darting around, attempting to see my surroundings. The gurney stops, a female nurse approaching me from the side. The male nurses leave the room, and she unbuckles the strap across my forehead. "You will behave while I remove your restraints, or I will sedate you."

I nod in agreement, and she quirks an eyebrow. "Yes ma'am." I concede. I'll do anything to prevent them from pumping me full of drugs. They fuck with my head, only aggravating my condition. Dr. Sweeney was adamant about keeping the sedation to a minimum as long as I played nice.

The straps around my wrists give way, and I wiggle my fingers to get the blood circulating again.

"My name is Nurse Carter. I will be assisting in your transition to Wellard Asylum." She slips her hand behind my shoulder blades, lifting me into a sitting position. She takes a step back, clasping her hands in front of her, staring down her nose at me. "The rules are simple, young lady. Do as you're told. Do not be disrespectful. Follow the treatment plan you're given. Do not cause any trouble. Do you understand?"

I nod. "Yes ma'am."

"Good. Now, I'm going to leave the room. Stay where you are. The doctor will be in to examine you."

She exits the room, closing the metal door behind her, the lock clicking into place. It's a deafening reminder of my situation, and I feel the finality settling deep into my bones. Now that I'm alone and unrestrained, I'm able to get a good look at my environment. The walls are concrete, the dull, gray paint chipping off in parallel lines, something dark outlining what looks more like claw marks the longer I stare at them. Squinting my eyes, I realize the deep color resembles dried blood. A chill slithers down my spine, and I shudder.

Why are people clawing the walls?

What the fuck is this place?

A cot is pushed against the wall, the once white sheets now a piss yellow color. Tilting my head back, the ceiling is covered in brown water stains, black mold spreading in the corners. The air feels damp and musty, my lungs beginning to reject the tainted oxygen in this tiny room. My gaze darts to the floor, filthy and covered in rat shit.

I'm going to die here.

Between breathing in fungus, and rodent droppings, I'll succumb to either respiratory failure or leptospirosis.

It's fitting, I guess. The penance for killing my family, even though they deserved it. The judgement wasn't meant for my hand, but I delivered it anyway. My only regret is not fleeing after I finished the job.

The latch on the door makes a terrible banging noise, the metal barrier swinging open. Nurse Carter reappears with a man wearing a white doctor's coat, a stethoscope around his neck. He appears to be in his early thirties, sandy brown hair, and dark eyes. Our gazes collide and his lips part, unnerving me to the point I want to shrink into myself. He's rather tall, well over six feet, his posture confident, exuding dominance. My eyes roam down his body, admiring his solid, muscular physique. While he may be good looking, there's something sinister about him that sets off alarm bells in my head. He blinks a few times, gathering his composure before stepping into my space, his white coat brushing the front of my knees.

"Hello Olivia. My name is Dr. Atlas Stone. I'm in charge of your rehabilitation here at Wellard Asylum." His deep voice commands my attention, and I sit up straighter as he speaks. "I've read through Dr. Sweeney's notes about your disorders. I know relocating facilities and changing physicians may be troubling, but I look forward to helping you in every way I can." He smirks, and a knot forms in my stomach, unsure if the tug of his lips is due to his genuine care of his patients or sinister intentions.

"Thank you," I respond meekly, just the way these people like me. While I may be the perfect patient, obeying every order, they have no idea what simmers just below the surface of my skin. There's a monster inside me, as Dr. Sweeney described when he saw me lose control. That's how he determined sedatives are not a good option for me.

"You've been diagnosed with Intermittent Explosive Disorder, Obsessive Compulsive Disorder, and Post Traumatic Stress Disorder due to physical and sexual abuse. You killed your father, stepmother, and stepbrother while suffering an IED episode. The court found you unfit to stand trial, and you were sentenced to a psychiatric hospital for a minimum of twenty years. Does that about cover it?"

"Yes." I agree, keeping my answers short and sweet.

He looks doubtful, clearly underestimating me, and my temper. With his cocky demeanor, I'm sure he'll find out for himself. He seems like the kind of prick that will push me to my limits just to see if I'll break.

The joke's on him. I won't be the one to shatter.

"Nurse Carter, you may leave." He dismisses her, his eyes never leaving mine.

"Yes, Dr. Stone." She nods, exiting the room, pulling the door until it's barely ajar.

He moves closer, planting his large frame between my legs. His hands on either side of my upper thighs, pressing into the thin cushion of the gurney. "Listen to me very carefully, little doll. You'll do what I say, when I say, or you will be punished." One hand reaches for my face, trailing his large fingers down my cheek. "I'm your God, now." He leans in, his face uncomfortably close to mine. "As long as you're a good girl, you and I will get along just fine."

My body trembles at his words, and I read between the lines. I'll be his fucking puppet, and he'll be my master. I want to claw his fucking eyes out. I killed my family because my father beat me, my stepmother hated me, and my stepbrother raped me. After three years of rehabilitation, I saw a glimmer of hope for myself. Now, it feels like I've been snatched back into my past, another man doing whatever the fuck he wants to me with no consequences.

My shoulders deflate, and I'm filled with hopelessness once again, knowing I can't fight a doctor at a mental asylum. The little voice in my head hasn't made a sound since I was last sedated. With it gone, I'm alone, making way for the depression and despair to take over, my compliance easily secured by whoever demands it. Meeting Dr. Stone's gaze, I nod my acceptance, my defeat making him grin.

"You're a gorgeous little doll, aren't you? So young and delicate. I'm no fool, Olivia. I've read every word in your file. I know you have a monster inside you. Rest assured, mine is bigger and more ferocious. I know what induces your episodes, and I know what brings you out of them. I can be your ally or your tormentor. It's your choice."

My breath hitches, realizing I'm in actual hell. I wish I

could bring on an IED episode now, so I could rip his fucking head off, and end this shit show before it begins. "I understand."

He pulls away, smiling victoriously. "I'm glad we're on the same page. I'll give you today to acclimate to your new home. We'll resume your treatment tomorrow."

CHAPTER TWO
OLIVIA

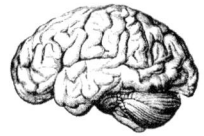

S hooting up on the bed, I'm disoriented, searching the darkness for something familiar.

My damp gown sticks to sweat slicked skin as I try to remember where I am. The thin mattress beneath me has reality slowly coming into focus, the humid, moldy air reminding me exactly where I am. Running my fingers through my hair, I let out a shuddering breath, trying to calm my racing heart. The room is dark with no windows, and I have no idea what time it is.

You're okay.

I tell myself over and over, adding an extra period to the phrase, so my psyche gets the even number it craves. My mind begins to calm, my breaths coming slower and more even, and I think back to yesterday's events. I'm in a new facility with a new doctor. There's a chance he may be a pervert, but he's *definitely* an asshole.

I thought the room where I met him was going to be my permanent residence, but I was wrong. Nurse Carter came back in after Dr. Stone left, leading me to the bathroom. I realized after seeing a "no entry" sign along the way, I'd been placed in the isolation ward. When I asked why I was being isolated from other patients, she glared at me, giving no response. I understand I have a volatile disorder, but I did fine at the previous hospital, never having issues with other patients. I kept to myself majority of the time, but at times, I found the background noise of the other patients comforting.

Here, there's only silence.

The one time I lost it in front of Dr. Sweeney was due to the sedatives I was given. I don't like being unconscious. It's a trigger for me, most likely a trauma response from the first time my stepbrother raped me. My biggest fear is having no control over what people do to me. Still, I don't think that's cause to keep me in isolation.

The banging sound from the latch draws my attention to the metal door. It's pushed open, Nurse Carter walking in with the same sour expression as yesterday. "Good morning, Miss Sterling. How did you sleep?" She asks flatly, and I know she doesn't give two fucks how I slept on this thin cot, the springs protruding through the overused mattress, digging into my body. Glancing across room, the only other accommodations are a toilet and a sink.

This is a prison cell.

"Fine. Thank you," I reply, shoving down my previous thoughts.

"Dr. Stone has requested you bathe before your appointment this morning."

"Will there be other patients in there?" I ask. The shower and bathroom areas at the previous facility were communal, but nurses always stood watch in case anything happened.

"No. Although all the patients in this ward use the same

area, we do not allow you in there at the same time. It is called the isolation ward for a reason, Miss Sterling."

Not trusting myself to keep the smartass retort to myself, I nod.

"Follow me. While you're showering, I will bring in clothes." She leads me to the bathing area, halting at the entrance. "Off you go."

She watches me closely as I hesitantly move inside the room, my eyes darting from one side of the room to the other. The open space has yellow lighting, every wall covered in calcium stains, the odor of mildew overpowering.

"I don't hear water running, Miss Sterling. Hurry up!" The nurse's impatient voice echoes through the room, and it snaps me into motion. Removing my white gown and white, cotton underwear, I place them on the sink. A few feet away, the shower head hangs from the wall, and I turn the knob, waiting a few moments for hot water that never comes. Grime covers most of the holes in the head, the stream of water spraying in all different directions. Gritting my teeth, I dive under the ice-cold water, my breath hitching as it beats against my skin. Glancing to the side, I see a small bottle of dishwashing detergent and a new bar of soap.

Great.

I might as well shave my head because my hair won't survive without conditioner. It sounds bratty to complain about something so trivial while I'm trapped in this hell, but even the previous hospital had fucking conditioner.

In record time, I scrub my hair with the detergent and my body with the bar of soap. They both smell terrible, and it's one more thing chipping away at my humanity. I'm a woman, but I've been used for a man's pleasure, thrown into a mental institution when I fought back, and quickly stripped of any feminine pleasantry most people take for granted. Before my mind can spiral any further, I turn off the shower spray and snatch the towel from the sink, courtesy of Nurse Carter.

How I missed her sneaking in here, I'm not sure. My eyes must've been closed to endure the frigid temperature of the water. My body shivers as I move the towel over my body, wrapping it around my hair once I'm dry. I slip on the clean underwear she brought in, and pick up the fresh gown, focusing on the little blue shapes adorning it.

"Hurry, Miss Sterling. You don't want to keep Dr. Stone waiting."

I startle at the sound of her voice, using the gown to cover my body as if she hasn't already seen me. "Yes ma'am." I quickly guide the garment over my head, the rough material scratchy against my skin on its way down, coming to rest right below my knees. Removing the towel from my head, I turn towards her as she moves further into the room. "Nurse Carter, do you know where my things are from the previous facility?"

She cocks an eyebrow, fisting her hips. "What things?"

"I had a toothbrush and toothpaste, deodorant, lotion, and a hairbrush."

She rolls her eyes. "We don't primp here, Miss Sterling. Your things were given to Dr. Stone. He will let you have them as he sees fit."

There are no mirrors in this room, but I imagine my hair looks like a rat's nest sitting on top of my head. I don't see how brushing your hair and teeth is considered primping, but I keep my mouth shut, sliding my feet inside the white slippers she's provided. I spot a hamper next to the wall, and I toss the towel and my dirty garments into it as I follow her out.

The hallway in this part of the building is different from where I came in. It was bright and blinding where this is dark and creepy. I stay close to Nurse Carter as I look at each door, counting them in my head to calm my nerves. The metal doors have a covered slot in the middle, just big enough to slide a tray through. I think about what kind of people are trapped behind each door.

Are they truly criminally insane?

Murderers? Rapists?

Or are they like me?

A product of their environment deemed unfit for society and already forgotten.

We reach the end of the hall, the nurse knocking loudly on a door that looks different from the rest. It's wooden, less secure, and more inviting.

"Come in."

Nurse Carter opens the door, nodding her head for me to go inside. As I cross the threshold, Dr. Stone sits at his desk, and I stop in front of it, my hands clasped behind my back. The door clicks behind me, and he looks up, a bright smile lighting his face, it almost looks genuine.

Almost.

His words from yesterday echo in my mind, and I know I have to be on guard around him.

"Olivia, good to see you." He stands, making his way around the desk, heading for the door. He flips the lock into place, his eyes finding mine as he turns around. He tilts his head to the side, eyeing me with interest. "Is something bothering you?"

He's being less of an asshole than yesterday. Maybe it was a scare tactic to keep the patients in line. I'm sure some of them are difficult considering some of them are truly depraved. Intimidation upon meeting him could deter bad behavior, but honestly, it just pissed me off. I don't want any problems while I'm here, so if I have to eat a little crow to keep him happy, I'll play the part.

He watches me expectantly, and I remember he asked me a question. Not sure how to answer, I reply with the first thing that comes to mind. "Nurse Carter said you have my things." I point to my unbrushed hair, and he smirks.

"I inspected your belongings of course to make sure you didn't have anything prohibited. What specifically do you need?"

"I would like it all, but if that's a problem, I'd like my deodorant, hairbrush, lotion, toothpaste, and toothbrush. How do I get more when I run out?"

"You'll let me know."

Exhaling slowly, I'm grateful for the use of basic hygienic products. "Can I have them now? I just took a shower, and if I don't brush my hair, I might as well shave it off. I don't know how it'll survive without conditioner." His eyes darken, and I fear I've said something to upset him. "I'm not a brat trying to primp, I only need the basics."

The side of his mouth turns up. "I see Nurse Carter gave her opinion. I'll make sure you have your things when you shower in the mornings."

His smirk gives me pause, and before I know it, I'm returning the expression. Maybe Dr. Stone isn't that bad. "Can I ask you another question?"

"Of course."

"Why am I in the isolation ward? I was with the other patients at the other facility."

He hums. "That was my doing. You're new here, and I'd like for you to get accustomed to your new surroundings before letting you into the communal areas. Your disorders are triggered, and I want to understand what we're dealing with before I introduce you to the other patients."

The logical part of my brain understands, but I still find it unsettling. "No disrespect, but I don't think sitting in a dark room with only a cot is going to help me. I'd think it would drive a person mad."

He motions for me to sit on the couch, and I obey as he pulls up a chair in front of me, sitting so close, the fabric of his slacks brushes my skin. "It's part of learning your triggers,

Olivia. I know this isn't sitting well with you, but I have a reason for everything I do." He places his hand on my knee, and I think back to yesterday, when he invaded my personal space, calling me his little doll.

His thumb draws circles just above my knee, below where the hem of my gown stops. The sensation is different, and while he didn't ask for permission, I find I don't mind the contact. I'm fully aware I can protect myself once I'm pushed to a certain point, the other part of my psyche taking over. But in my *normal* frame of mind, I'm uncomfortable with people invading my personal space, touching me.

Dr. Stone is hard to get a read on thus far, but my instincts are telling me he's safe for the time being. "Will I stay locked in my room?" I whisper, staring at my hands in my lap to avoid eye contact. He's making me nervous.

"You'll spend some time with me every day. You've just transferred, and I want to ensure you receive the best treatment. I've transferred some of my patients to other doctors, making sure I have plenty of time to focus on you and your needs."

Something tightens in my stomach, and I dismiss the feeling immediately. He's the complete opposite of Dr. Sweeney, and I wonder if I jumped to conclusions about him yesterday.

He squeezes my knee, capturing my attention as he grins. "Do you have any hobbies?"

I shrug. "I like to read, but they told me I couldn't bring my books with me when I came here."

His brows furrow. "I'm sorry, Olivia. It's protocol. What genre do you like to read?"

My face heats. "Anything really, but my favorite is horror and romance."

He chuckles, leaning back in his chair, taking the heat from his touch with him. "Interesting."

I grin, my cheeks heating under his assessing gaze. His eyes darken, and I look around the room, taking in his office. I'm sitting on a black leather couch matching the leather chair he's currently occupying. His desk is dark mahogany, literally filling half the space, a Victorian style chair behind it. The walls are covered with shelves, hundreds of books lining them, and my fingers twitch, the desire to touch every one of them overwhelming. The far wall has a closed door and a large window next to it, sunlight filtering into the bright room. It's a welcomed view after the hours I sat in darkness yesterday.

Glancing to my left, I gasp when my eyes land on a gynecological chair, the stirrups extended, a tray lined with tools beside it.

He notices my reaction, and there's a sudden dip in the cushion beside me, his warm body pressing against mine. "I'll be your doctor for every need you have, little doll. I'll treat your mind, body, and soul."

I swallow thickly, my mouth suddenly dry. His hand comes to rest on my thigh, over the fabric of the gown, and I shiver. "I've never had that done."

He tilts his head to the side. "You're twenty years old. You've never had a gynecological exam?"

I shake my head, my face heating with embarrassment.

His fingers grip my chin softly, turning my face to his. "Don't hide from me. I'm going to take care of you."

This man is fucking dangerous, his promises alluring, and I feel something tighten deep inside my chest.

I can't trust my instincts.

I cared for my stepmother and stepbrother in the beginning.

I loved my mother and father.

But here I am, locked in a fucking insane asylum because I protected myself.

The justice system failed me.

An underage girl being physically and sexually abused was okay, but defending myself wasn't.

Dr. Stone is being nice to me, and that's why I'm reacting this way. It means nothing. In the end, he'll betray me too.

Just like everyone else.

CHAPTER THREE
OLIVIA

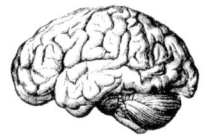

My routine has remained the same since I arrived a week ago.

I'm greeted every morning by Nurse Carter's sour expression and shitty demeanor. Meals are brought to my dungeon, and I sit on the floor, the stream of light from the slot in the door illuminating the food. I usually only take a few bites, enough to sustain me since I don't know what the fuck I'm eating.

After each meal, I'm taken to Dr. Stone's office for my therapy sessions. It seems a little excessive, but I don't mind the company. Our conversations hadn't delved into anything significant or traumatizing until yesterday. He'd read Dr. Sweeney's notes in my file, but he hadn't asked for any details about what happened. It's strange. We had only talked about common things, like two normal people having everyday conversations. But our last session yesterday left me raw and vulnerable.

After three years, I felt no remorse as I recounted the night I murdered my family. While they deserved their fate, I find the brutality I'm capable of to be both jarring and concerning. It's as if someone else takes over my existence when things become too hard. I'll never understand why I didn't kill my stepbrother the first time he raped me, or the dozens of times after. I've never made sense of why my mind chose that night to kill my family, but I wish the switch would've been flipped sooner.

At first, Dr. Sweeney thought I may have multiple personalities, but he quickly dismissed the theory after he witnessed one of my episodes. He said I responded to my own name, never revealing a second identity. While I do hear a voice when an episode is coming on, he described it as the devil on my shoulder, not an altered consciousness.

Whatever is wrong with me, it's ruined my life, and I'm stuck in this fucking place for another seventeen years.

The latch sounds, alerting me to Nurse Carter's arrival. I'm sitting on the cot, my back leaning against the wall. I'm about to move off the thin mattress, but as I look up, a man I've never seen stands in the doorway, his hateful gaze burning a hole into me. My body tenses as he steps into the room, his energy causing my anxiety to skyrocket. "Get up, Sterling."

My hackles rise at his harsh tone. "Who the fuck are you?"

He lunges forward, backhanding me so hard, the side of my face bounces off the concrete wall before my body crashes to the mattress.

I groan as my vision dims, but a clinking, metal sound in the distance startles me, and I scream. "No! You're fucking dead! I killed you!" My stepbrother's bloody face comes into view, shards of glass protruding from his face as he unbuckles his belt. His eyes darken, making his sinister intentions known as he saunters towards me.

"He's baaaaaaack!" The voice sings in my head. "Kill him!"

His hands land on the mattress on either side of me, his large form crawling up my body. My feet come together as I lift my legs, kicking him in the chest as hard as my cramped position will allow. He stumbles back, his hand flying out, the wall steadying him as a loud roar fills the room. "You fucking bitch!" He runs at me full speed as I slide off the bed, darting behind him. Thrusting my palms against his back, I send him crashing into the concrete wall above the cot. He bounces backward, falling to the ground, a crunching sound alerting me something is broken.

Gripping the edge of the mattress, I throw it across the room, screaming so loudly, my throat burns with the force of my rage. Pulling on one of the metal springs from the cot frame, I twist it back and forth until the rusted metal snaps from the pressure. My stepbrother lies on the ground, holding his head with his hands, groaning in agony.

"Finish him!" The voice demands and I giggle, thrilled I have the opportunity to kill him again. I pounce on him like a panther, straddling his hips, pressing the metal spring against the side of his throat. His pulse thunders against my fingertips, and I long to feel it fade away once again. Pressing the sharp point into his throat, the skin pops, a spray of blood showering my face. "Did your cock grow back, stepbrother? Do I get to cut it off again?"

He tries to rip the spring from his neck, but I press deeper, ensuring I drain his blood completely this time. Just as I move to put my knee in his balls, a sharp sting shoots through my neck, and before I can see who's attacking me from behind, I slump forward, and everything goes black.

There's someone sitting on top of me.

They're trying to suffocate me.

The pressure in my head, and the burning in my chest has my strangled lungs desperately gasping for air. My eyes snap open, and Linda stands before me, calling me a liar and a whore. Raising the fire poker behind me, my arm freezes mid-swing, the air around me suddenly pressurized and suffocating.

"Olivia! Calm down!" My father's voice pierces my eardrums, and I fight the resistance, doing everything in my power to knock his ass out with the iron rod in my hand.

"Fuck you!" I grit out, the throbbing in my head almost too much to withstand. "I'll kill you again just like I did your beloved, rapist stepson!" I shout, laughter bursting from my lips as I try to move my limbs, but the air previously restraining me has morphed into leather straps. "You had to tie me down because you know I'll kill you again. Fucking coward!" I snarl, his face becoming blurry, and a wave of dizziness crashes into me.

"Olivia."

"Shut the fuck up!" I roar, but the voice calling my name sounds different this time. My eyes snap shut, fighting the nausea churning in my stomach.

It's a trick. It's a trick. It's a trick. It's a trick.

"It's Atlas, little doll. Your father is dead."

Little doll. Little doll. Little doll. Little doll.

"Count with me," Atlas says. "One."

Atlas? I think he's Dr. Stone. Yes, Dr. Atlas Stone.

I know him. "One."

"Good girl. Two."

"Two." My fingers begin to tap the side of my thigh as I

continue counting along with him, his gentle voice soothing my rage.

He says a number, I repeat the number. We do this back and forth until he reaches ten.

Thank you for ending on an even number.

My body relaxes as I take a few deep breaths, my raw throat working slowly to produce some much-needed lubrication. Opening my eyes, Dr. Stone's concerned gaze penetrates mine, and I know I'm fucked.

"They're dead," I whisper, fighting the tears trying to escape.

"They're dead," he states. "So is the orderly you managed to kill with a cot spring." I swear he's fighting a smile, and that should concern me, but it eases the tightening in my chest. "Tell me what happened, little doll."

Holding his gaze, I sniffle. "Can you scratch my nose? It's itching."

He chuckles, raising his fingers to do as I asked. He watches me for a moment before undoing the leather restraints. I glance down.

Velcro, no metal.

He remembered.

Metal belt buckles trigger my PTSD, which triggers my IED. The sound is forever ingrained in my memory because of my stepbrother. Every time I heard the noise, it was like an alarm going off, letting me know he was about to rape me.

Nurse Carter enters the room, gasping. "Dr. Stone, I don't think you should release her!"

His gaze remains on me as he speaks. "Good thing you don't get paid to think, Nurse Carter. Leave the room and close the door behind you."

She glares at his back, huffing out her frustration before exiting.

"Tell me," he demands.

I sigh. "He came into my room being rude. I asked who he

was. He backhanded me and unbuckled his belt. The switch flipped, and here we are."

"Why did you wake up in a rage?" He asks, his brows furrowing.

"Dr. Sweeney figured out the hard way I don't react well to sedatives. He didn't put that in my file?"

He shakes his head. "I'm sorry about that, but I'm looking into different ways to calm you down during an episode. You had a spring in his neck, bleeding him dry. I don't think counting was going to help." He grins this time without trying to hide it.

"Shouldn't you be upset or horrified?"

He winks. "I'm not your typical psychiatrist." He stands, holding out his hand. "He deserved it anyway." I take his hand as he pulls me up from the cot, brushing his thumb across my lip. "He got you good, little doll."

"I got him back."

CHAPTER FOUR
OLIVIA

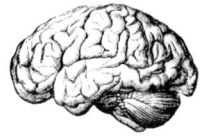

Nurse Carter doesn't speak a word as she opens the door, glaring at me with disgust. She steps to the side, silently demanding I follow her like a puppy going outside to take a piss.

I follow her down the hall to Dr. Stone's office where she leaves me at the door. I knock quietly, before opening the door, noticing a paper gown lying across the couch. My head whips to side where he sits behind his desk.

"I'm going to perform your gynecological exam today." He stands, coming around the desk. "Go into the bathroom and change into this." He hands me the thin garment. "The open side is for your front." My lips part, but he doesn't budge. "Go, Olivia."

He seems agitated, and it catches me off guard. I knew this day would come, but I thought I'd have more time. I hardly know this man, and he's about to see me naked. Maybe he's had time to think about yesterday, and he's decided it was my fault after all.

Once I'm in the bathroom, I change into the paper gown, pulling it closed as tightly as possible. The material rips from my grip, and I sigh. *Fuck.*

Opening the door slowly, I find he's waiting for me. "Climb onto the chair and place your feet in the stirrups."

I'm unable to meet his gaze, so I turn quickly, lifting myself onto the chair. The paper rips again as I hold it together in a death grip as I lay back, securing my feet in the stirrups. I'm completely mortified, naked with my legs spread, my most intimate parts open for him to see.

This feels wrong.

He comes to my side, stroking my fingers, loosening the firm grip I have on this paper shit I'm wearing. "I'm going to perform a breast exam first. This is designed to check for any abnormalities in your breasts. Next, I'll move to your vagina for the pap smear. The exam requires me to insert a speculum inside you, which will separate your vaginal walls. I'll use a spatula to collect a sample of cells from your cervix. You may feel a little pressure or discomfort, but that's normal. Once I finish, I'll insert my fingers while applying pressure to your abdomen, which allows me to check your uterus and ovaries. Do you have any questions before I begin?"

I'm gaping at him like a fish out of water. This sounds like a lot of shit I want no part of.

He senses my panic, trailing his cool fingers down my cheek. "Trust me, you'll be okay. Just lie back and let me do what I need to."

Squeezing my eyes shut, I let out a long breath, nodding my agreement. I may have to feel it, but I don't have to see it.

My body jolts like I've been shocked as his large hand palms my left breast. His fingers probe around, and my cheeks heat as my nipples harden. Goosebumps erupt across my skin, and I wish I could crawl in a hole and die.

"It's a normal reaction. Don't be embarrassed." He chuckles.

That's easy for him to say. Not only are my hard nipples on display, but my core is also soaked, and I pray my arousal doesn't drip onto the chair beneath me. This is the furthest thing from normal I've ever experienced.

This is so fucked up.

He pinches my nipple between his fingers, and I gasp. "Did that cause any discomfort?"

Quite the opposite. Not trusting my voice, I shake my head.

He shows my other breast the same attention, and I expect the sensation this time when he pinches my nipple. What I didn't expect was his warm breath against my ear. "Such a good little doll."

My breath hitches as his heat quickly disappears, leaving me a cold and trembling mess. Opening my eyes, he's sitting on a stool between my legs, a silver tray loaded with tools next to him. My core clenches at his closeness, and time stops as he just sits there, staring at my pussy, his tongue licking a trail across his bottom lip.

Kill me now.

My mind wanders far away from what's happening until my attention snaps back to the cold, metal tool probing at my entrance. My hands ball into fists at my sides as he slides it inside, spreading me open once it's fully inserted. Something scrapes against my insides, and I wince.

"The worst is over." He reassures me, and I exhale.

He stands from the stool, and the click of a cap sounds too loud in the quiet room. Cool liquid meets my entrance, and I freeze as his finger slides inside me. My lungs stop functioning as it slips out of me, and he adds another finger before thrusting back in. My lower belly coils tightly, and the strange sensation is foreign, but not unwelcome.

I've never had an orgasm; my only sexual experiences

were forced on me against my will. The abuse disgusted me to the point I didn't even touch myself. Now, I'm being examined by my doctor, and I feel like something is building inside me. "Dr. S-Stone."

"Hmmm?" He hums, watching as his fingers glide in and out of me.

"Um, I've never, I don't know what's happening." I pant, his fingers pushing deeper, my eyes rolling back in my head.

He pauses, and as I meet his gaze, I'm staring at the devil himself, dangerous and starving. He bites his bottom lip, and I clench around him, a whimper escaping my lips. He groans, his fingers moving in and out of me slowly. The hand on my stomach moves lower, his thumb pressing against my clit. My hips jerk off the chair, and a moan slips past my lips, the intense feeling almost too much.

He finds a torturous rhythm, his fingers and thumb working in tandem, bringing me to a cliff I'm not sure I'm ready to dive off of. As his fingers plunge deeper inside me, he applies more pressure to my clit, and I explode, pure pleasure crashing into me, bright stars colliding behind my eyelids. My body contorts in a way it never has, and he pins me down with a hand on my stomach, while he slides in and out of me, dragging every ounce of pleasure from my body.

"Atlas," I whimper.

He pulls his hand away, and I shudder at the loss of him. Opening my eyes, he's at my side, smirking. "Did you enjoy that, little doll?"

I nod. Fuck yes, I did.

"If you're a good girl, I'll give you more."

I gasp, my eyes squeezing closed, not entirely sure what he means by that. Does he mean more of what we just did, or does he want to have sex? Could I have sex without freaking out? Without being reminded of my stepbrother? My mind whirls with all the possibilities, and the consequences of a doctor and patient fooling around. I descend into a downward spiral, but before I'm completely lost in the chaos my mind creates; warm lips press to mine.

My eyes snap open for a moment, before fluttering closed once again, his tongue tracing the seam of my lips. I open for him immediately, losing myself in his warmth, and the dizzying feeling from his tantalizing rhythm. He slips his hand behind my head, pressing us closer together, growling in the back of his throat. The sound makes me shiver in his hold, his mouth becoming more demanding, voracious. His free hand slides beneath my back as he lifts me, and I wrap my arms around his neck, my legs around his waist. He spins around, pushing me against the wall, his hard length pressing against my core. His lips trail across my jaw, nipping and sucking the sensitive skin of my throat.

"Atlas." I'm breathless, lost in a haze of lust. *What the fuck is happening right now?*

"Feel what you do to me, little doll?" He groans, grinding his cock between my thighs. A moan slips from my lips, and his fingers dig into my ass. "I'm trying to be a gentleman. Those little noises you make are proving that difficult."

I sigh as his warm breath caresses my ear, his tongue darting out, licking a tantalizing trail down the side of my neck. Tilting my head, I give him better access. "Does a gentleman usually make his patient come during a gynecological exam, Dr. Stone?"

A deep growl rumbles from his chest, and I yelp as he nips my earlobe. "Watch it, little doll. I haven't shoved my big cock in your tight cunt yet. I consider that *very* gentlemanly." My mouth falls open and he chuckles, closing it with a finger under my chin. He kisses me once more before loosening his grip, my body sliding down his muscular form.

As my feet touch the floor, he cups my cheek in his palm, our gazes colliding. "You're beautiful, Olivia."

My cheeks heat as I look anywhere but at him. Things have changed between us today, and I'm not sure what that means. Of course, the orgasm was amazing, as was his talented mouth. But he's my doctor, and I don't need any more complications in my life. I don't want him to lose his job either.

He taps me on the nose with his finger, pulling my attention back to him. "Get out of your head. No one knows what goes on in this office but us."

My eyes widen. "D-do you plan on this happening again?"

He smiles wickedly. "I have so many plans for you, little doll."

CHAPTER FIVE
OLIVIA

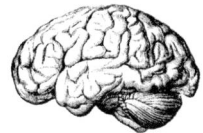

"Do you have a home?" I ask, sitting on the black leather couch, waiting for our session to begin today.

He looks up from his paperwork, tilting his head to the side. "I do. Why do you ask?"

"Just curious. It seems like you're always here."

"I have a home in the country, but I stay here most of the time due to the long drive. There are a few spare rooms available in case the doctors need to stay overnight."

"Oh." I'm not sure where I was going with this.

"Is there anything else you'd like to know about me, Olivia?" He smirks, and my stomach flutters.

I bite the inside of my cheek. "You spend a lot of time with me. Doesn't it cut into your time with other patients?"

"I've transferred a few of my patients to other doctors. Your treatment is my top priority. You have a chance at a life outside this hospital, and I want to make sure you receive the help you need."

My chest tightens. He seems like he actually cares. "Thank you," I whisper.

He looks down at his paperwork once again. "Change into your examination gown. It's in the bathroom, hanging on the back of the door."

My heart damn near beats out of my chest. Silently, I rise from the chair, quickly entering the bathroom, closing the door behind me. Taking a deep breath, I push the ill-fitting fabric over my shoulders. It falls down my body, hitting the floor, my white, cotton underwear following closely behind. Reaching for the paper gown on the back of the door, I slide it over my shoulders, the front hanging open. Standing in front of the mirror, I truly look at myself for the first time in a long while.

My hair is long, the red and orange color looking dull and lifeless. I used to think it was strawberry blonde, but I'm not quite sure what color you'd call it now. When it's shiny and full, it's beautiful and wavy, but now, it's straight and thin. My skin is pale, my green eyes full of pain and sorrow. The bags beneath them are dark and hollow, my cheeks sunken in as if I'm malnourished. I do eat a little, but the food here is a mystery most days. I usually taste test before every meal, when they shove it through the slot of my door. If I don't gag, I eat it. I've lost some weight since arriving at Wellard Asylum, but my body is still appealing. Too bad I can't say the same for my face and hair.

Taking one last look in the mirror before opening the door, I sigh, heading back into the office. Atlas is standing, leaning against his desk, arms crossed in front of his chest.

"On the table."

Climbing onto the cushioned table positioned next to the gynecological chair, I sit straight as a board, my heart thumping in my chest. He hasn't touched me since my last exam, where he made me come for the first, and only time in my life. I've tried multiple times in the last week to bring myself pleasure the way he did, but it never comes.

I never come.

He pushes off the desk, crossing the room and halting in front of me. "You seem like you're under the weather, little doll. I'm going to listen to your chest and examine your throat."

My brows furrow. "I don't feel sick."

He smirks. "Better to be safe than sorry."

"I have to be naked for this?"

His jaw clenches as his hands move to his waist. My body goes rigid, expecting to fly into a rage as soon as the metal clinks, but the triggering sound never comes.

Meeting his gaze, his eyes soften. "I took it off before you came in."

My chest constricts, grateful tears threatening to fall. I've never met anyone so considerate, so understanding. He's my doctor, and what we're doing is wrong, but I want him.

He unbuttons his pants, sliding down his zipper, pushing them down his thighs along with his briefs. All the air rushes from my lungs as my eyes land on his huge fucking cock. My lips part, a tightness coiling in my lower belly, and I'm not sure if it's excitement or fear. Maybe a little of both.

His fingers grip my chin, lifting my face up to his. He pulls a bottle from his back pocket, flicking the lid open, squirting clear liquid into his palm. He palms his thick cock, spreading the lube over himself, slow and steady, his eyes darkening.

I'm conflicted about so many things in this moment. The only other person I've had sex with forced himself on me. The emotional scars of having my innocence stolen by a family member is something I've never truly dealt with. Killing him brought me a measure of peace, but the memories continue to haunt me.

While I want Atlas, my anxiety spikes, terrified I'll slip into one of my episodes if he does something unintentionally triggering me. I meet his gaze, allowing him to see my trepidation.

"Keep your eyes on me." He steps between my legs, his thumbs moving slowly to spread my pussy open. He bites his bottom lip, his cock sliding along my slit, working himself back and forth, and I grip the table, my head falling back on a gasp.

He fists my hair, forcing me to look at him. "Eyes. On. Me." He growls, pushing himself inside me.

The burning stretch is too much, and it feels like he's going to rip me in half. "Atlas. It's too much."

"Relax, little doll. I'm not fucking you today. You're just keeping my cock warm while I examine you."

My brows furrow because I don't understand the pleasure in that, but I don't dare question him. I'm uncomfortable, too full, and stretched beyond my limit, but I won't risk saying anything to cause him to change his mind. The longer we're like this, I realize there's pleasure in pain, and I want to experience it.

With his cock buried impossibly deep inside me, he raises the end of the stethoscope to my chest. He listens intently as I remain quiet, attempting to think of anything other than his dick just hanging out inside my pussy.

The reprieve is short lived as he leans back, standing at his full height. His hips punch forward, a scream tearing from throat. His hand flies to my mouth, his lips pressing against my ear. "Quiet, or someone will hear you being my little slut." My face flames at his words, and he smirks, removing his hand slowly. "Open wide."

I stretch my mouth wide, and he leans forward, shining the light down my throat. The shift of his body causes his hips to pull back, giving me some relief. He takes his time looking inside my mouth, and my jaw begins to ache from holding it open.

"Your throat looks good," he murmurs, his hips punching forward as his hand flies to my mouth once again. He rubs my clit furiously, and just when I think I can't take anymore, my body explodes. This is so much more intense than using his fingers.

It's fucking life altering.

My entire body burns with the pleasure racing through my veins, and my back arches, pushing him deeper inside me. My vision dims, but not in the way of an oncoming episode. Little bursts of light peek through the darkness, a feeling of euphoria tingling across my skin.

Trailing his nose up my neck, he whispers against my ear. "Filthy girl. Coming around your doctor's cock while he examines you."

Something snaps inside me, and I reach up, gripping the back of his neck, crashing our lips together. I pull him forward as I lean back, grinding my sensitive pussy on this cock.

He growls as my tongue sweeps inside his mouth, taking what I want. "I said I wouldn't fuck you today," he grits out, and I nip his bottom lip. He breaks the kiss, his piercing, dark eyes penetrating me just as deeply as his cock. "Fuck it."

He grips my hips, and I wrap myself around him as he walks us over to the couch, tossing me onto the plush cushions. He sheds his clothes quickly, and all I can do is stare at his toned body, biting my bottom lip. He lowers his body on top of me, sliding inside me easily thanks to my orgasm moments ago. "You're fucking trouble." He groans, gripping my ass, tilting my hips so he can slide deeper. "So fucking tight." I swear I feel him in my womb, and when I whimper in both pain and plea-sure, he grips the back of my head, burying my face in his neck. "Bite me to quiet those sexy fucking noises you make."

My tongue darts out, licking the salty musk from his skin, making him groan, his strokes becoming harder and deeper.

I know I'll be sore. I'll have bruises. But I can't bring myself to care. My mind is quiet, nothing strong enough to penetrate the world he's created for us.

I'll do anything to stay in this place.

He circles his hips, rubbing himself against my clit as he thrusts inside me. I can't stop the desperate pleas escaping my lips, so I do the only thing I can to muffle the sounds. I sink my teeth into his neck as the most mind-blowing orgasm hits me, stealing the breath from my lungs. He growls menacingly like an apex predator as I cling to him, the metallic taste of blood filling my mouth. "Harder," he demands, gripping my hips painfully, pounding into me like I'm nothing more than his little fuck hole.

My teeth sink deeper, the copper taste of blood overwhelming my taste buds. He grunts, his strokes becoming erratic, more punishing. My body reacts, pulling tightly like the string of a bow, and just as he buries his face in my hair to muffle his release, I come again, crying out against his skin. His hips slowly rock into me, dragging out our combined orgasms as I rake my nails down his back.

His body shudders as he lifts his head, his gaze locking onto mine. "There's no escaping me, little doll. You're mine."

"Yes, Dr. Stone." I agree, licking the remnants of his blood from my lips.

CHAPTER SIX
ATLAS

I'm fucking obsessed.

Jesus Christ.

I knew the moment I laid eyes on her, she would be mine. Now that I've had her tight pussy wrapped around my cock, she'll never escape me. She's drawn my blood, and soon, I'll draw hers.

Earning her trust has proved to be an easier task than I originally thought. Long conversations and comfortable silence. Kindness with a firm hand. I easily provide all these things based on what she needs. Throw in some charm and a few orgasms, and I just about have her where I want her. Her faith and complete submission are what's needed for when the true torture begins.

I want her pleasure, but more, I want her pain. *Her rage.*

Her murderous side to come out and play. *More.*

She killed an orderly with a fucking metal spring.

I almost came in my pants when I walked in her room, the fire-haired goddess on top of him, not a care in the world other than killing the threat.

Fucking beautiful.

She needs a safe environment to unleash the killer inside her. I'll provide that for her, encourage the morally corrupt behavior. Release all her sinful desires, the ones she tries to bury deep inside her soul. Once she's free, not a care in the world, I'll shatter her into a million pieces. Break her beyond repair, reshaping her into the woman I want her to be.

Call it diabolical. Call it *evil.*

Either way, Olivia Sterling belongs to me until the day she takes her last breath.

Even her death will be on my terms, by my hand.

Not a moment before. I'll fight the fucking reaper for her soul. Fate guided her onto the path of murdering her family, carefully weaving the intricate threads leading her to me, her destiny.

She was institutionalized at seventeen. She spent three years under the care of a fucking quack before he did the world a favor, and retired. He didn't help her. He gave her a comfortable space where she could hide instead of owning her trauma, using it to overcome her disorders. None of that matters now. The universe has delivered her to me, and I'll push her until she breaks.

At twenty years old, she suffers from Intermittent Explosive Disorder, Obsessive Compulsive Disorder, and Post Traumatic Stress Disorder. The PTSD triggers her explosive episodes. The OCD keeps her mind focused at times, bringing her out of the episodes. Other times, she's too far gone, and sedatives are needed to stop the tantrums. I find it intriguing she wakes from the sedation in an episode. Dr. Sweeney never mentioned that in his notes, only a small note scribbled on a therapy session journal advising against further use of sedatives.

Her brain decides when she's allowed to return to her normal psyche, and God help anyone who crosses her path before that happens. The devastating combination of all three disorders would destroy anyone.

Not *her*.

She's strong as fuck, and stubborn. But I can help her be *more*. If anyone is capable of breaking her, *it's me*.

She's permitting the rage and PTSD to control her, constantly terrified of having an episode. She refuses to consciously allow her demons to play, let them consume her, unleashing her hell into the world.

Releasing them onto *me*.

I'll embrace her wrath, show her how to withstand it, mold it. She'll hate me, and I'll enjoy every fucking second of the fight. I look forward to the challenges I'll face with Olivia. It'll be quite refreshing compared to the mundane life I live.

Growing up, both my parents worked in the mental health field. My father was a renowned psychiatrist, specializing in bipolar disorder and schizophrenia. My mother was a nurse at a juvenile behavioral center; rehabilitating adolescents diagnosed with mental health problems. Due to their professions, my childhood was ridiculously boring. Both my parents observed me constantly, analyzing every word I spoke, every move I made. I often felt as if I were on display, trapped in a glass cage. Their clinical approach to their work spilled over into our family life. They weren't affectionate people, nor complimentary. No matter how well I excelled, how proficient I became, there was always room to improve.

Nothing was ever good enough. *I was never good enough.*

Once I graduated high school, I decided to go into psychiatry. It's not so much I enjoy helping people with their problems. I enjoy digging into their psyche, discovering what makes them tick. If I help them along the way, good for them. If not, I really don't give a shit. It's become a dull existence, the same thing day in, day out.

It's slowly driving me insane. *Ironic.* I've held out hope that one day someone will come into this asylum, capturing my attention. Someone to captivate me, show me something fascinating I haven't seen a thousand times before.

At thirty-four years old, my life is empty other than this fucking place. My parents died a few years ago in a fatal car accident. Their death didn't affect me the way it probably should've. I felt nothing for the people who brought me into this world, the parents who raised me. After I moved out, and went to college, we didn't communicate much. They were always suspicious of my behavior, recommending I should be evaluated due to my lack of emotion. While I may not share the sentiments and feelings of the average person, I feel the blame should be placed on my sterile upbringing. Love and comfort were absent in our home, and I find it absurd to expect something from a child that you never taught them, much less gave them.

I have no siblings or extended family, none that my parents mentioned anyway. They never discussed their past or their own parents, but I was the one who needed help. They refused to look in the mirror and recognize *their* disconnect with the outside world.

Shortly after graduating college, I took a job as a mortician while I interned at a mental health facility. I needed money to pay the bills, and I enjoyed working with the dead. The profession was low-stress and enjoyable, no endless chatter about feelings and expectations. The corpses were a finality I admired, an end to whatever suffering or misfortune they had while living, but I didn't have to hear about it. It was done, and they were guided to the darkness, existing in whatever awaits us after death.

A chance encounter at the cemetery one night changed my financial status significantly.

A man approached me from the shadows, offering a way to make fast cash if I could keep my mouth shut. Little did I know, stealing organs from cadavers and selling them on the black market would set me up for life. While every corpse wasn't eligible, depending on how long they were expired by the time we received them, I moved quickly on the bodies that arrived immediately from the hospital.

No one suspected a thing.

Taking the job at Wellard Asylum, I had to give up organ trade. Dealing with the living was disappointing, but financially, I had already made all the money I'd need to live a very comfortable life.

Once I'd established myself as loyal and trustworthy, Dr. Halstead confided in me.

Patients never leave.

If we can't control them, we dispose of them, the manner in which that happens is of no importance. It's truly survival of the fittest here, and if you're weak, you'll be euthanized, and I'll collect a hefty amount of compensation for your organs.

Simple.

But deep down, I know my little doll is a survivor, and I have every intention of proving it. I'll teach her how to survive in this hell, though I'll be the devil in her story. The villain she'll come to despise, the man she'll need above all else.

Wellard Asylum is an unsanctioned hospital, meaning there's no government agencies or programs overseeing it. It's privately owned, therefore Dr. Halstead can run the place however he sees fit.

I've heard many rumors about him since I came here. Some of the whispers lingering in the halls say he was a patient at Wellard during his teenage years after killing his entire family. They claim he changed his name, earned a degree, and took over as the main psychiatric doctor immediately after Dr. Ravine died. I find it hard to believe a previous patient would be in charge of this facility, but stranger things have happened in the few years I've been here. While those particular statements may be rumors, there are things I've seen with my own eyes, things I took part in. Participating because it interested me or simply to earn his trust.

Halstead has a hidden basement inside the asylum; one he uses for his own research in new treatment options for the criminally insane. He subjects patients to sensory deprivation, lobotomies, and my personal favorite, electroconvulsive therapy. I've been present, looking on as he performs transorbital lobotomies, a truly fascinating approach to altering the way a brain processes emotion.

I find sensory deprivation to be effective, but it takes a while for most patients to react. I'm a fan of instant gratification, so this method doesn't appeal to me as much as electroconvulsive therapy. It's instant stimulation used to subdue the person's brain functions. It has certain side effects if performed often, but used sparingly, it will help the patient with their mental illness.

Knowing Olivia will require certain treatments has a bolt of excitement shooting through me. The plan I've come up with has me thinking outside the box, and a little deprivation might just be what my little doll needs.

CHAPTER SEVEN
OLIVIA

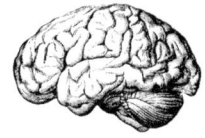

I'm so fucking confused.

I've come to depend on him for comfort and support, yet he's left me alone in this fucking hole, like I'm nothing.

"Stupid fucking girl." The voice in my head screams as I realize I've once again put my trust in someone who doesn't deserve it. He toyed with me and got what he wanted. At this point, I wouldn't be surprised if he does the same thing with all the other female patients. I have a migraine from all the back and forth in my head. I make excuses for him, then I tell myself I'm nothing more than a plaything, a warm hole to stick his dick in.

Why do I keep doing this to myself? What happened with my family should've taught me a hard lesson, but for some reason, I refuse to learn.

You can't trust anyone but yourself.

"You seem agitated today." His voice breaks through my thoughts.

He had Nurse Carter bring me into his office fifteen minutes ago. He didn't bother looking up from his paperwork, only pointing to the couch for me to sit.

Bastard.

"You're keeping me in the isolation ward. At least in gen pop I could talk to people."

"You make it sound like you're in prison."

My jaw clenches. "Oh, I'm sorry. I didn't realize this was a play date."

"Olivia, you know I don't care for sarcasm."

"Respectfully Dr. Stone, fuck you." Damn. I'm on a roll today.

His dark eyes meet my gaze, his jaw clenching so tightly, I'm surprised his teeth don't shatter. "What the fuck did you just say to me?"

I know I should take it back, smooth things over, but I'm not in the mood today. Uncrossing my legs, I lean forward, my elbows on my knees, enunciating each word slowly, adding volume to my voice. "I. Said. Fuck. You."

He opens the top drawer of his desk, removing something I can't see. Rising from his chair, he makes his way towards me, a sadistic grin on his smug face.

My eyes dart to his right hand, a syringe dangling from his fingers. "Atlas, no!" I scream, jumping from the couch.

His devious grin widens, his perfect, white teeth gleaming in the sunlight filtering through the window. My stomach churns, bile teasing the back of my throat.

One.

Two.

Three.

Four.

With every step he takes, I retreat quickly, a twisted dance of survival, a predator circling his prey. "Atlas, stop! You can't sedate me. I won't fucking let you!"

That was the wrong thing to say.

He growls, accepting my determination as a challenge. "Little doll, when will you learn? I can do whatever the fuck I want to you."

My heart lurches in my chest. The man I've come to admire, the one I've developed feelings for is just as sadistic as my step-brother. The realization freezes the breath in my lungs, my body going rigid. My vision dims in the corners, and my head spins, my mind on shuffle, looking for what I need to protect myself.

"Kill him." The voice snarls, and whether it's another consciousness or the devil on my shoulder, I'm in agreement with the bitch.

The doctor who's supposed to help me, give me another chance at life, is a fucking lunatic. He knows I can't handle sedatives. He's witnessed what happens. He doesn't care.

The slow simmer of rage barrels toward the surface, and there's no stopping it now. Whether he sedates me or not, he has a fucking fight on his hands.

Bracing my feet apart, he stops in his tracks, tilting his head to the side. "There she is. My vengeful, little doll. You make me so fucking hard when you lose control."

"Come play with me then, fucker." I grin, moving behind his desk.

He chuckles darkly, moving to stand on the other side, directly in front of me.

Wrong move.

Before he realizes it, I've jerked the keyboard from the computer, slamming it into the side of his head. He curses, stumbling back as I jump on top of the oak desk, lunging for him. He hits the ground hard with me on top of him, and I laugh manically in his face. "You like getting your ass kicked by a little doll, fuckface?" Rearing back, I don't give him the chance to respond before punching him square in the fucking throat.

He chokes, his coughing and gagging making me laugh harder. I don't want his pretty face to feel left out, so I throw my fist into his nose, blood instantly gushing from his nostrils. I continue pummeling him over and over, my knuckles splitting open, our blood mingling together, creating a beautiful shade of crimson.

Glancing beside me, a stapler lies out of place on the floor, and the voice is a caress inside my mind.

"Staple his lips together so he can't tell his pretty, little lies."

As I reach for it, I feel a pinch in my thigh, and I scream bloody fucking murder. The burn is immediate as he fills my veins with the knockout poison. My head slowly turns, and I glare down at Atlas. His white teeth are a stark contrast to the blood covering his face, trickling from his mouth, down his chin.

"Checkmate, little doll." His words are the last thing I hear before everything goes black.

CHAPTER EIGHT
ATLAS

L ifting my arms quickly, I catch Olivia before her pretty head bounces off of the hardwood floor.

I've been waiting for this moment.

To be the object of her rage is the greatest gift she could've given me.

I knew she was upset I hadn't sent for her in a few days. The entire plan was orchestrated with the intent of seeing her in her finest, most furious glory. Once I knew my plan was successful, all I had to do was give her an extra push.

I had no intention of sedating her, but she didn't need to know that part. The syringe was a prop to send her spiraling down the rabbit hole into madness. The only reason I sank the needle into her skin was because I knew she'd kill me if I didn't stop her. I can't allow either of us to stop breathing. Not yet.

There's too much fun to be had.

Fuck.

Every time her fist connected with my face, I almost came in my pants. She lunged for me like a rabid fucking animal, and my cock strained to be inside her while she beat my face bloody. A grin tugs at my lips, knowing I could've overpowered her at any moment, if only I wanted to. She played right into my hand, the excitement I feel only surpassed by the warmth of her tight cunt.

She may not be up for that afterwards.

Everything played out beautifully, my little doll the perfect opponent. She acted exactly how I hoped, giving me what I need to proceed.

Dr. Halstead approved my request for the equipment I need without batting an eye. He never reads medical inquiries, blindly approving everything we ask for.

Evil bastard.

He gets off on the pain and torture of patients. If it does them harm, he's all for it. Saying those things may seem hypocritical, but what I have in store for Olivia will mutually benefit us both. He craves suffering. I crave *her*.

Maybe I'll let Olivia kill him one day before we leave this place.

I've amended my plans to include getting her out of this place. The details have yet to come to me, but I refuse to accept Wellard Asylum as her home. I'm going to cure her, reset her. There's no way I'll be comfortable putting all this effort into her just to leave her here. It would be counterproductive to all my hard work.

As I approach the room where she's being held, I breathe deeply, centering myself. She'll experience pain now, but there's a larger picture she'll come to understand. I'll scramble her up a bit, molding her into an obedient little doll, just for me.

I'll save her.

Pushing open the heavy, metal door, I saunter inside with every bit of confidence I feel. Nurse Carter stands beside the gurney where Olivia is restrained. Leather straps bind her wrists and ankles, while another stretches across her forehead, pinning her head in place.

"Thank you, Nurse Carter," I say flatly. I can't stand the old bitch, but she serves her purpose in times like this. She's cold and heartless, her presence only spreading misery to the patients because she thinks they're nothing. She may not be as bad as Halstead, but I'll most likely kill her before we leave.

Olivia stirs at the sound of my voice, her eyes widening slightly in her heavily medicated state. She growls like a feral dog, jerking against the leather straps binding her.

"Calm down, Miss Sterling!" Nurse Carter shouts, and it causes my temper to flare.

"Do not speak to her, Nurse Carter. Just stand there and do what I say. No commentary needed," I grit out, and she takes a step back at my tone.

Turning my attention back to my helpless little doll, I smile. "Shhh, Olivia. Everything is going to be okay. Your trauma is holding you back, worsening your mental state. I'm going to help you."

She growls again, and if Nurse Carter wasn't standing beside me, I'd whip my dick out and stroke it until I'm coming all over her pretty face.

Later.

The gurney whines as she struggles against the straps, but it's no use. She's trapped.

In more ways than one.

Giving her my back, I focus on the electroconvulsive machine, flipping the power switch on, letting it warm up.

These days, doctors usually administer anesthesia before performing shock therapy. Here at Wellard Asylum, we believe the more you feel, the more it stimulates your brain to expel the disorder ailing you. Neither credible nor moral theory, it's how we do things.

My eyes shift to the metal head piece lying beside the machine. I wrap the ends with white cloth, dipping them into a metal bowl filled with cool water. Defibrillator gel is preferred, but water will work just fine. She may be left with scorch marks on her temples, but nothing too serious.

Facing my very angry patient again, I grin. She's so violent and hostile. So beautiful and unhinged.

The things I want to do to her.

"Would you like me to place the muffs on her head?" Nurse Carter asks, and a low growl rumbles deep in my chest.

"No. I don't want you touching her. Or looking at her. In fact, face the wall, Nurse Carter, until I tell you otherwise."

Her withered eyes widen, but she obeys, shuffling herself into the corner like a child.

My gaze finds Olivia, and if looks could kill, I'd be a dead man. "What the fuck are you doing to me?" She grits out, her voice rough and raw as if a demon is trying to claw its way out of her.

"I'm helping you, Olivia. This will ease the pain in your mind," I murmur, stroking her cheek with my fingers. She snaps her teeth, merely missing my hand, and I chuckle.

Reaching behind me, I lift the rubber mouth guard from the counter, attempting to place it between her teeth as she continues fighting the inevitable. Gripping her lower jaw, I press my thumb against her lower teeth, pushing down force-fully. After sliding the guard into her mouth, I remove my finger quickly, avoiding her vicious bite. She tries to spit it out, but I cover her lips with my hand, shaking my head. "You're going to need it to protect those beautiful teeth."

Her green eyes widen a fraction, all her fight halting momentarily. I'm not stupid enough to believe she's surrendering; this is the episode slowly receding. Her expressions allow me into her mind as the rage dissipates, realization and fear seeping into her bones.

Sliding the contraption over her head, the muffs settle tightly against her temples. She flinches, drops of cool water sliding down her clammy skin, disappearing into her hairline. Our gazes lock, and I see the terror in her eyes, the anxiety causing her body to tremble.

Don't worry. I'm going to fix you, little doll.

My hand finds the voltage dial, turning it up to one-hundred and twenty volts since this is her first treatment. Placing my finger on the black button that will send an electrical current through her brain, I catalog every emotion I can interpret in her emerald eyes.

Confusion. Fear. Hate.

She'll get no sympathy from me.

Can't she see I'm doing this for her?

Without another moment of hesitation, I press the button, sending pure electricity surging into her brain. The low hum from the machine buzzes around us as Olivia's body arches off of the gurney. The muscles in her neck strain against the skin confining them, her beautiful face contorting with agony. The mouth guard bulges at the edges, her beautiful teeth clenching in a death grip. Her entire body convulses, and I grin, knowing I've made the right decision.

This is exactly what she needs.

Pressing the button again, the current of raw energy ceases, and she crashes back to the gurney, her porcelain skin more pale than usual. She continues to tremble, her eyes squeezed shut, absorbing the glorious torture I'm inflicting on her sinful body. What felt like minutes were only a few seconds in reality. The longer the shock, the more likely she'd suffer brain damage. I only want to erase her trauma, not her mind completely. Long minutes pass before she slowly opens her eyes, immediately finding my gaze. My brows furrow at what I see.

Rage. Defiance. Hatred. *Murder.*

Shaking my head, I chuckle to myself. "Again."

CHAPTER NINE
OLIVIA

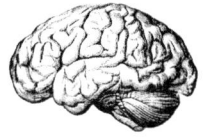

gain?

A What the hell is he talking about? Why do I feel like ripping his beating heart from his fucking chest? *"Kill him."* The voice whispers into my mind, sounding withered and broken.

The last thing I remember is sitting in his office, pissed off because he ignored me for days, leaving me to rot in solitary confinement. Glancing at my amused doctor, I'm startled by the dark bruises forming under his eyes, and a swollen nose with remnants of dried blood flaking beneath his nostrils. The image of Atlas stalking towards me with a syringe in his hand flashes through my mind, and I know without a doubt, I'm the cause of his injuries.

Fuck!

It feels like my brain is being slammed against my skull, and I wince at the pain in my head.

Everything hurts.

I move to cup my head, but panic sets in when my arm won't move. My limbs aren't working, and I can't move my head.

Am I fucking paralyzed?

He slips a hard object over my temples, and I shiver as cold water slides down my skin, soaking into my hair. It's then I notice something thick and rubber-like filling my mouth. "W-what?" It comes out garbled.

"Glad to have you back, Olivia. You're IED episode has earned you a punishment this time." He replies, the hint of a smile tugging at his lips.

"Why?" I try again, drool leaking from the corners of my mouth.

"You didn't play nice," he says with finality, as if his vague answer should explain everything. Without another word, he turns away from me. Before I take in my next breath, my body seizes, my back bowing painfully as agony like I've never felt assaults my body.

Fire.

The flames of hell rush through my veins, boiling my blood as if the sun itself is filling the vessel holding my consciousness. My muscles tighten; my core being ripped to shreds. A scream rises in my throat, but no sound escapes, my vocal cords stretched beyond their limit, along with the tendons in my neck. My hands and feet strain against the bindings, the leather biting into my skin. My jaw clenches, the thing in my mouth saving my teeth from grinding into dust. Darkness appears at the corners of my vision, and just as I succumb to the lightning bolts piercing every molecule of my being, the electricity surging through my body stops.

As I come to, the gurney whines, wheeling me down the low-lit hallway. It takes every bit of willpower I possess to open my eyes, and I'm truly terrified as I stare through the two tiny slits. The world around me is blurry, confusing, and bleak. My limbs protest as I try to shift, restraints holding me securely in place.

The rolling, metal bed comes to a stop, a loud metal door being pushed open.

What the fuck is going on?

My lips part to ask the question firing on repeat inside my head, but my tongue won't move. My mouth is dry, and my throat feels so raw, as if I've swallowed a handful of rocks. Or sandpaper. I'm wheeled into a room, two sets of hands working to remove my bindings. I want to fight them, ask why I feel like this, but I can't do anything except groan a garbled plea, begging for this horrible feeling to go away.

Suddenly, I'm lifted off the gurney, tossed onto a bed like a bag of garbage. My head bounces off the concrete wall, pain exploding throughout my skull. I cry out, the strain of my voice adding to the excruciating agony behind my eyes.

"Oops." Someone chuckles.

"No matter," a woman replies flatly. *Nurse Carter.* "She won't remember anyway."

Before I can figure out what she means, a sharp prick digs into the skin on my bicep. She backs away quickly, the needle releasing from my muscle. My eyes droop immediately, and I'm fighting to hold onto consciousness. The voice in my mind, the one that usually lingers, demanding I fight and protect myself is nowhere to be found.

There's only silence.

I'm truly alone.

"Get out!" A voice snarls, and goosebumps erupt across my skin.

Footsteps scurry across the concrete floor, and a large presence moves closer to my bed. He gently moves my hair, inspecting the area that hit the wall, and I wince.

The clicking of his dress shoes is the only indication I have he's retreating from the bed, crossing the room. My mind is shutting down, my eyes still closed as I drift into the void of darkness.

"Sleep, little doll." It's the last thing I hear before the clanking of the metal door closing.

Atlas.

CHAPTER TEN
ATLAS

She's sleeping.

Curled up in a ball on her bed, she's facing the wall, breathing deeply.

At my request, Nurse Carter gave Olivia a low dose sedative, just enough to help her sleep through the night. The old bitch knew better than to question me, especially after I saw how rudely she was deposited into her room. I told her if she hurt Olivia again, she'd be the next body on a gurney.

I'll kill that cunt before we leave, little doll.

The door creaks as I push it closed, careful not to latch it. She doesn't stir as I cross the room, carefully lying down beside her.

This fucking bed is terrible.

Snaking my arm across her middle, I pull her back against my chest. Her limber body comes easily, the deep sleep holding onto her tightly. Burying my face in the crook of her neck, I breathe in her scent. She smells of sweat, fear, and the promise of slow death. My tongue darts out, licking her salty skin, my eyes closing as her flavor bursts across my tongue.

My cock hardens, my body aching to take what belongs to me. Gripping the hem of her gown, I slide it up her body, gathering it around her waist. Hooking my finger into the cotton material, I slide her panties down her thighs, past her calves and her toes, letting them fall onto the mattress. Lifting her leg, I rest it back over my hip, my hand sliding to her pussy, parting her lips slowly. Between the trauma she suffered today, and the state of her deep sleep, she's as dry as the fucking desert.

Bringing my fingers to my lips, I suck them into my mouth, getting them nice and wet. Slipping them between her legs again, I circle her clit with my thumb, sliding my lubricated fingers inside her warm cunt. My eyes close at the feel of her, and I begin to thrust in and out of her, wishing she were awake to clench around me.

My breathing picks up as her pussy becomes wetter, her sleeping form responding to my touch. "That's it, little doll. Even in your sleep, your body craves me."

A soft whimper escapes her throat, and everything inside me perks the fuck up. My fingers plunge deeper, and her body shifts, pulling her leg forward, rolling onto her back.

"At-las." She breathes, still asleep.

Fuck.

I've come to sacrifice my belt around Olivia, so I make quick work of unbuttoning my pants, pushing them down my thighs. Lifting myself off the shitty mattress, I climb over her, holding my weight on my forearms, my body pressing against her. Leaning down, my tongue traces her lips, before kissing her softly. Her lips are dry and cracked, but I don't mind. My cock jerks as I notch it at her opening, pushing inside her achingly slow.

It's torture.

It's hell.

It's all fucking consuming.

Her breath hitches, her eyebrows pinching together, but she doesn't wake up. While I'm enjoying taking my time, watching each expression cross her sleeping face, I have an overwhelming need to fuck her hard. I want my cock to rip her from the darkness she's trapped in.

My hips surge forward, punishing her swollen pussy for making me feel this way. Damn her for crawling her way under my skin. I grit my teeth, pounding into her over and over, knowing she'll feel the result of my obsession tomorrow, and the day after.

Her lips part as I use her body for my own pleasure, not an ounce of remorse for the unconscious doll beneath me. Over and over, I drive into her, savoring the soft noises she can't contain even in her sleep. My eyes dart to her neck, and the memory of my blood on her lips flashes through my mind. My balls tighten, my cock swelling thicker, harder.

I clench my jaw to stay in control as her inner walls clamp down around me, an orgasm barreling through her, a deep moan escaping her lips. That's all it takes. I crash my lips to hers, muffling my groan as I fill her tight little cunt full of my cum.

Ensuring she receives every last drop, I drive into her one final time. My eyes land on her face, her furrowed brows relaxing once more, the medication doing its job perfectly. I slide out of her warmth, rising to my knees, trailing my index finger over her clit, to her dripping hole. My cum leaks from her, and my jaw clenches. Scooping it up with two fingers, I lean over her, gently trailing it across her lips.

One day I'll take your mouth, little doll.

The thought of her pouty lips stretched around my cock has me hardening again. Battling the urge to fuck her a second time, I rise from the bed, pulling my pants up, straightening my clothes. Reaching for the blanket, I stretch it across her body, tugging it up to her chin. She's truly breath-taking, a natural beauty many women pay good money for.

How can this violent, tiny girl look so fucking fragile?

As I exit the room, I give her one last glance over my shoulder. "See you tomorrow, little doll."

CHAPTER ELEVEN
OLIVIA

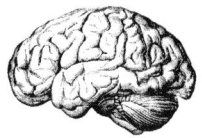

My eyes slowly open, and I feel like I've been hit by a bus.

Everything aches, and my head is throbbing. Bringing a weak hand to my temple, I wince, my lips parting as my fingers graze the tender skin. Something crusty falls onto my gown, and I slide my fingers down to my mouth, finding my lips caked with some kind of residue.

What the fuck?

Using the collar of my gown, I scrub my lips roughly, removing all traces of the substance. I don't think drool does that once it's dried, but I've been in a deep sleep for an unknown amount of time.

Bracing my forearms, I push my upper body off the mattress, scooting backwards I'm sagging against the wall. I frown as my leg brushes a damp spot on the sheet.

Did I piss myself?

Running my fingers across the wet fabric, I realize it's creamy and sticky, as well as the inside of my thighs. Glancing towards the end of the bed, my panties lay tangled in the sheet, and anxiety creeps in.

What the fuck happened to me?

Confusion has me tapping my fingers on the outside of my thigh, and I lose my train of thought as memories flood my muddled mind.

Arguing with Atlas in his office.

Slipping into an episode, the details just out of reach.

Strapped to a gurney, electricity surging through my body like a live wire, my entire existence rebelling against the foreign energy lighting me up from the inside out.

My heart rate spikes as I relive tiny flashes of torment. I search for more details, but an invisible wall slams into me, blocking my prodding. The fear of the unknown has me spiraling, my chest constricting, a thin sheen of sweat coating my skin.

One.

Two.

Three.

Four.

"I've got you." The voice whispers so faintly, it sounds as though it's carried on a nonexistent breeze through the darkness. My chest loosens a fraction, and my breaths come a little easier.

The door opens, the metal scraping across the concrete floor like a piercing bolt to my head. Nurse Carter strides in, her face sour as ever. "Let's go, Miss Sterling. You must shower before your appointment with Dr. Stone."

Shifting my body, it takes me a few moments to find my bearings before standing from the bed. Meeting her gaze, I ask, "What happened to me?"

She scoffs as if I've asked the most ridiculous question. "You had one of your tantrums. You were punished."

Memories of my limbs seizing and pain ricochetting through my veins flash through my mind, and I flinch. I don't utter another word to the cold bitch.

Pushing myself off the mattress to stand, I take a moment to compose myself before following her out of the room. She leads me into the shower, placing a fresh gown and toiletries on the sink. "Hurry up," she snips before exiting the room, and I step under the cold spray, the temperature throwing me back onto a gurney with frigid hardness pressing against my temples.

"You're okay," I tell myself. Concentrating on the bar of soap in my hand, I scrub my body the best I can. Most places are hard to reach with the current state of my muscles, but I grit my teeth, powering through the discomfort.

Once I'm finished, I brush my teeth and hair, sliding on the clean gown and cotton panties. It swallows me whole. I've lost more weight since arriving at Wellard Asylum, and my head hangs in sorrow, realizing this is where I'll finally break down and wither away. Any hope I had of receiving help with my disorders and a future living a normal life is slowly disappearing. The road ahead looks bleak, surrounded by fractured memories, rough concrete, and impenetrable darkness. Foolishly, I believed Atlas would be my saving grace. I thought there was something between us. I latched onto the idea, placing my faith in a man that says all the right things.

I know he did this to me.

My memories may be broken, but I remember him being there.

I remember the fucking pain.

He hurt me.

I don't understand how he could do this.

What will I do now?

Leaving the shower area, I meet Nurse Carter in the hall, the silent tension suffocating as the clicking of her heels echo around us. We reach Atlas's door, and she knocks impatiently.

"Come in," he shouts, and my stomach churns.

The old cunt spins on her heels, walking away as I twist the handle, pushing the door open slowly.

"Have a seat on the couch, Olivia."

Closing the door, my anxiety spikes, and I count my steps to the couch.

One.

Two.

Three.

Four.

Another step could've been taken, but my fourth step is larger, so I end on an even number. Staring at the floor, I keep my gaze down as I sit on the plush, leather cushion in the middle of the couch.

"Were you counting?" He asks, and I nod. "Are you upset?" I nod again. He sighs, rising from his chair, coming to squat down in front of me. "Look at me and use your words, Olivia."

I meet his gaze, my teeth grinding together. "What do you want me to say?" I grit out.

His jaw clenches. "Calm yourself. I don't want a repeat of yesterday."

A humorless laugh bursts free before I can stop it. "Seeing as I don't remember much, I'm not sure I can change the outcome of today."

"What do you remember?" He asks, his hands coming to rest on my thighs as he sinks to his knees.

I ignore the heat flooding my core as his fingers brush across my sensitive skin. "We got in an argument."

He tilts his head to the side. "What else?"

"Pain," I sneer, pushing his hands from my legs.

His head hangs as he sighs, almost as if he feels guilty.

"You were upset yesterday. You had an episode and attacked me. I had no choice but to sedate you."

My mind catches up, allowing me to take in all the bruising on his face, remorse weighing heavy in my chest. *I did that to him.* "Why was I upset?"

"I've been busy, and we went a few days without seeing each other. You were angry, then I was angry, and it snowballed from there." He meets my gaze, and emotion flashes in his eyes, but it's gone before I can decipher what it is. "It was out of my hands. Dr. Halstead took one look at me, and ordered corrective action be taken. I had to perform electric shock therapy on you." I gasp. "I'm sorry, Olivia. I didn't want to do that to you, but he gave me no choice." His head hangs again. "Please forgive me."

My chest tightens at his words, and I lean forward, cupping his cheek as his eyes meet mine. "You didn't want to hurt me?"

He shakes his head. "Of course not." He searches my face. "Are you okay?"

"No," I whisper.

He grips my hand, pulling me to my feet. He leads me into the bathroom, spinning me around to face the mirror. My breath rushes out of my lungs, and I'm horrified at my reflection. Leaning forward, I quickly spot the reason for the sensitive skin on my temples.

Burns.

I don't dare touch them, already feeling the constant sting since waking up. Examining myself further, I don't miss the black circles under my eyes, the sunken cheekbones protruding from my pale face. There's no mirrors in the community shower area, a safety precaution, I'm sure. They don't want us killing them when their backs are turned. I can't say the idea of sinking a piece of glass into Nurse Carter's throat has never crossed my mind. Pulling the gown tightly around my waist, I'm shocked by how much weight

I've lost. I've felt thinner, the gown growing larger and heavier, but I look terminally ill.

Disgusting.

Unhealthy.

I meet Atlas's gaze in the mirror; his expression filled with concern.

"I don't look like me anymore," I whisper, a sense of loss hollowing my chest.

He takes a tentative step forward, hesitating only a moment before wrapping his arms around my waist, pulling me back into his chest. "You're fucking beautiful, Olivia. I won't hear anything different."

My chest heaves. "Could this happen again?"

He nods.

"I can't control the IED. How is punishing me like this anything other than torture?" I ask, my eyes fixed on his in the mirror because I can't stand to look at my own reflection any longer.

"It's designed to either teach you to control your disorder or banish it completely."

"That's ridiculous," I grit out. His words unsettle me further, and I'm instantly worried if we keep talking about this, I'll lose my temper, which is the last thing I need right now.

His gaze darkens for a moment, and I bite my tongue, praying the voice inside me stays silent.

"Come." He spins me around, leading me back into his office, seating us on the couch. "What do you need from me right now?"

I ponder his question, no clear answer springing to mind. I need the fucking pain to go away. I need to *not* lose myself in this concrete prison. I need out of this place.

Realizing I must've said the words out loud, he shakes his head. "You won't lose yourself, little doll. You'll hold onto me. I know it's hard to hear this right now, but I need you to trust me. Can you do that?"

How the fuck am I supposed to trust him when he's the one doing this shit to me? The decision may come from the top, but it's insane he'd go along with it. He'll lose his job if he doesn't do what he's told. You could end up with someone worse. *Much worse.*

Does it get worse than this?

I don't like either side of the coin, but Atlas seems to care about me. He's my only chance at surviving this place. He watches me carefully, and I nod. "I'll try."

He blows out a breath, his hand coming up, his fingers stroking my cheek. "I've missed you."

His words shatter something within me, and I lean into his touch. "You're all I have, Atlas."

He leans in, his thumb trailing across my bottom lip. "I'm all you need, little doll."

I attempt to steady my breathing, my heart racing at his closeness. "Your face looks terrible. I-I'm sorry."

One side of his mouth tugs up. "Are you saying I'm no longer attractive, Miss Sterling?"

I smile at that. "You're okay, I guess."

He pulls me onto his lap, and I wince. "I'll give you something for the pain, sweet girl."

I twist my fingers together between our bodies. "Will it sedate me?"

"No. It only blocks your pain receptors." He assures me, pulling my forehead to his.

"That would be great."

His mouth inches closer, our breaths mingling together. "I'm barely hanging on here, Olivia."

My stomach flips. Pressing my lips to his, he groans, carefully pulling my body tightly against him. My aches and pains fade away as his mouth devours me, slowly, methodically. His hands slide down my back, gripping my ass, grinding me against his slack covered cock. I moan into the kiss, my body coming alive beneath his touch. "Atlas."

He pulls away, his eyes darkening as he watches me. Cool, calculating, a predator assessing his prey. His lips curve up slowly, his pupils blowing wide, unmasking his desire. "Lay back on the couch and spread your legs. I'm about to eat you alive, little doll."

CHAPTER TWELVE
ATLAS

Watching her break down at the sight of her reflection did wonderful things to my cock.

Honestly, I was hoping it would send her into an episode. My face is bruised and sore, but fuck if I don't want her tiny fists to draw my blood again. I want to see the split skin of her knuckles bust open, her blood mixing with mine. My cock leaks pre-cum at the thought of our combined lifeforce filling my mouth, and I groan.

She's shattering before my eyes beautifully, losing all hope, abandoning her faith in everything.

Except me.

I'm her lifeline. Her saving grace. *Her God.*

Everything is falling into place perfectly.

She's unhealthy, depressed, and alone. She hardly eats enough to sustain her. She's starving physically and emotionally.

Just the way I want her.

When the final wall crumbles in her mind, ripping her apart at the seams, I'll swoop in, solidifying her obedience and loyalty to me. *I have a plan.* Our future is already written, and as she plays into my hand, all will be revealed. She believes my rehearsed emotions, my practiced expressions. I didn't get where I am today without discipline and dedication. My well executed charm is winning her over, and soon she'll be my own little puppet.

Doing as I say. Being the woman I want her to be. *Mine.*

She climbs off my lap slowly, lying back on the couch, spreading those gorgeous legs wide. I lick my lips, pure lust slamming into me. While my emotions may be a façade, my desire for Olivia is the one truth I can't deny. I need her body, her submission, her fucking soul. Winning her heart along the way will make the process easier, but it's not required.

I shift on the couch, hovering above her frail body. Lifting her gown over her breasts, I take in her delicate form. While hunger is necessary in this stage of the plot, I've already concocted a plan to remedy the issue, returning her to full beauty, to good health.

Just another way to bind her to me.

My lips trail over her protruding rib cage, licking a path down her sunken abdomen, sliding the patient issued panties past her slender thighs. She gasps as I bury my face between her legs, breathing deeply, past the flowery smell of the soap, my cock jumping at her natural scent.

So fucking addictive.

Pushing her thighs further apart, I swipe at her clit with my tongue, sinking two fingers inside her, deep. Her body arches, and my cock throbs knowing she's in pain, but she just can't help herself. Pulling her clit between my lips, my teeth graze her swollen bud, and she moans deeply as my fingers find her g-spot.

"I'm so close," she whimpers, and I smile at how responsive she is to my touch.

I groan as her inner walls clamp down around my fingers, her thighs clenching around my head. She slaps a hand over her mouth just as she reaches her peak, her body bowing as she loses control. I continue sucking her clit, finger fucking her through the orgasm, and as she relaxes against the cushions, her legs trembling, I finally pull away.

Her eyes open slowly, glazed over with satisfaction. Crawling up her body, I press our lips together, shoving my tongue between her lips. "Taste yourself, little doll. You're fucking delicious."

One of the few truths I'll share with her.

She pushes herself up, the hint of a smile on her lips. "What about you?"

I lift myself to a seating position, patting my thigh for her to take her place on my lap, where she belongs. She crawls on top of me, straddling my hips, wrapping her arms around my neck. Her dripping cunt leaks onto my slacks, and I grin as she unknowingly marks me with her scent.

"I'd love to sink my cock inside your pussy, but I don't think your body can handle it right now." She opens her mouth to object, but I press a finger to her lips. "I don't think your throat could take me either." I quirk an eyebrow, daring her to disagree.

She nods, and I brush the hair from her face. After the beautiful way she screamed for me yesterday, I know her throat is raw. I'm a depraved motherfucker, but I'm not cruel enough to fuck her throat now.

"What do you want to do?" she asks, her worried gaze finding mine, and my cock twitches.

"I've extended your therapy sessions. After what happened yesterday, I convinced Dr. Halstead I need more time in order to rehabilitate you." Her eyes widen, and I stifle a grin. "I have a lot of paperwork to catch up on. Are you tired?"

She nods.

Kissing her deeply, my tongue mimics what my cock should be doing to her cunt. She grinds down on me, and I'm momentarily sidetracked, moving her soaked pussy back and forth across my lap. She moans, snapping me back to reality, and I grip her hips, placing her on the cushion next to me. Rising from the couch, I stalk towards my desk, grabbing what I need from the middle drawer. Lifting a bottle from my desk, I head back to the couch, holding the water and pain medication in front of her. "Take this and get some rest. I'll wake you when it's time to return to your room."

She reaches for both, popping the pill into her mouth, chasing it down with the water. She lays down on the couch, turning onto her side, so she can see me as I work.

Crossing the room to my desk, I take a seat in the chair, ruffling some papers in front of me. Halstead doesn't give two fucks what we do with these patients. I could move her into my office, and he wouldn't blink an eye. But she doesn't know that.

My eyes dart to hers after a few minutes, noticing they're already closed. The medication hasn't had time to kick in, but I know she's still exhausted from yesterday. I place the stack of papers next to the computer, as if I'm entering information. Bringing up the start menu on my desktop, I find what I'm looking for, settling back in my chair.

Solitaire.

I could've stayed on the couch with her. I could've given her the affection she craves. But as I begin playing the game, easily filling the rows, wasting time as she sleeps, I reinforce my decision.

It's all part of the plan.

CHAPTER THIRTEEN
OLIVIA

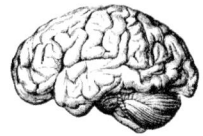

While the high of an orgasm is incredible, it only lasts for so long.

The loneliness and pain always creep back in.

It was after dark when Atlas woke me up, leading me back to my room. It was nice staying with him while he worked, the first time in a long while I've actually felt content.

While he was the one who executed my *punishment*, he didn't orchestrate it. I can't fault him for following orders to keep his job. Still, there's something heavy in my stomach, a deep pit, telling me something is really wrong with this place.

I'm curled up in a ball on the paper-thin mattress when a scraping noise captures my attention. It sounds like nails digging into the concrete.

The orderly didn't close the slot on the door when he brought my food earlier. A stream of light shines into the dark cell, and I follow its trail until my eyes land on a hole at the bottom of the adjacent wall. I watch it for a few minutes before a tiny little head peeks out into the open room.

My body uncurls slowly, careful not to spook the little rodent. He surveys the area before the rest of his body appears, his long whiskers twitching as he sniffs the air around him. Reaching for my tray at the end of the bed, I use my index finger to scoop a dollop of the slop from the bowl they provided for dinner. Quietly as possible, I hang my hand over the side of the bed, wiggling my finger until the glob drops onto the floor. The smacking sound spooks the little guy, and he darts back into his hole.

My stomach sinks with disappointment, and I sit silently, staring at the dark void for any sign of his return. A few moments pass before he cautiously reemerges, heading straight for the questionable food. He gobbles it down like he's starving to death, and I slowly reach for more of the mystery dinner, let it slide down my finger, onto the floor.

He jumps back, but he doesn't run this time, making me smile. "Hi."

He flinches, glancing up at me with beady little eyes. His whiskers twitch as his nose works overtime, trying to catch my scent.

"You're a cute little guy. Too skinny, but cute. Come see me every night, and I'll fatten you up. Okay, buddy?" He lets out a squeal, and I huff a strained laugh, accepting the delusion this rat can understand what I'm saying. "I'll call you Gus."

He stands up on his hind legs, sniffing the air again, his front feet dangling in front of him. I grab the tray with the food, placing the entire thing on the floor. Gus runs, but he returns quickly, climbing into the bowl, his tiny feet disappearing beneath the slop. He spins in a circle eagerly, gorging himself, and I smile at how happy he is. Warmth fills my chest knowing I provided that for him, along with a full belly.

Quietly as possible, I lay back down on the mattress, resting my cheek on my hands. Gus twirls round and round, cleaning the bowl, and my eyes droop as the exhaustion of the day settles over me. "Goodnight, Gus-Gus."

I shoot up in bed, my hand flying to my chest.

A stream of light filters into the room, and it takes a few moments for my eyes to adjust. No one ever closed the slot on my door. Scanning the lowly lit room, I try to figure out what woke me up. It wasn't a nightmare this time.

"Please!" A male begs, and I flinch at the desperation in his voice.

Slowly slipping from the bed, I creep towards the door, sinking to my knees once I reach the metal barrier. Rising just enough for my eyes to see through the slot. The door across from my room is open, and I squint, not sure what I'm looking at.

There's a long, narrow, rectangular box inside the room. It's hollow, with metal slats around the sides every few inches, four legs raising it a couple of feet off the ground.

"No! Please! Let me out!" The man sobs, and I gasp when I realize he's inside the box, his fingers darting through the slats, reaching for something, though I'm not sure anything can help him at this point.

What the fuck is happening?

He's lying on his back, and as I watch the orderly close the lid, I shudder at the tight fit. The man can't move. The click of the lock makes my stomach churn, bile rising in my throat. My vision blurs, tears stinging my eyes as I listen to the man's pleas, witnessing his fight against the confinement. It's like shoving a large dog into a small kennel.

"Mr. Henderson, calm down," a familiar voice coos, and the sweetness of his tone makes the little hairs on my arms stand up.

Atlas.

He steps forward from where he was hidden, his tall frame blocking my view of the man.

"I didn't do anything! It was a nightmare!" The man, Mr. Henderson, cries out. "Please let me out!"

Atlas circles the contraption, and I get a side view of his profile. His sandy brown hair is perfectly styled, his gray dress shirt and black slacks impeccable. He's dressed for success and completely at ease as he watches this poor man suffer in a fucking adult crib.

"This is all part of your therapy, Thomas. We've installed the Utica crib in your room for this purpose. Your claustrophobia is debilitating, and we're working to help you overcome it."

I've never seen Thomas Henderson's door open before. I've never heard so much as a peep from the other patients in this wing since I've been here. At times, I thought I was the only one inside the isolation ward. Knowing there are other people here, suffering, is horrifying.

"I'm better, I promise! Please let me out!" Thomas sobs, and I can't look away as he claws at the metal slats, desperate for freedom.

"Let's go, Henry," Atlas instructs the orderly. "You can resume your duties. I want to check on Miss Sterling."

Before I can duck my head, dark eyes meet mine, and a sinister smile lifts his lips. I'm paralyzed, unable to move or look away from his penetrating gaze. Warning bells go off in my head, and my instincts tell me I'm fucked.

The orderly closes the door across the hall, muting Mr. Henderson's screams, striding away after clicking the lock into place. Atlas bends down, his eyes filling my vision through the rectangular slot. "Hello, Olivia."

CHAPTER FOURTEEN
ATLAS

The door latches behind me as I enter the room, and I pat the keys inside my pocket before slowly prowling towards Olivia.

She retreats until the back of her knees hit the edge of the bed, her body rigid as she sits on the mattress. "What is that thing?"

My initial reaction was to be angry she found one of my favorite pastimes. Just as quickly as the it flared, it vanished. She's a curious little thing, and I'm dead set on pushing her boundaries. "It's called a Utica crib. We use it to calm patients who are out of control."

Her face pales, realizing the implications of what I said, and I grin.

Yes, little doll. You'll fit in one too.

"He said he had a nightmare. He wasn't out of control. He was just scared." She counters.

"That may be true, but he suffers from severe claustrophobia, and the crib works wonderfully to help work through those fears."

"Sounds like it," she sasses, and my cock twitches.

I come to a stop directly in front of her. "What was that?"

She tenses, her head falling back to meet my gaze. "It doesn't sound like it's helping. He's terrified, Atlas."

Olivia has a soft heart and good intentions, but it's a weakness that will get her nowhere in this place, or in life. She needs to toughen up, let her rage take over, shifting her into an impenetrable force who can survive anything.

That's where I come in.

I'll mold her into the person she needs to be, by any means necessary.

My hand shoots out, wrapping my large fingers around her slender throat. She gasps, and I push her down onto the bed, crawling over her thin body. "Do not question how I treat my patients. It can easily be you in that box."

Her pale skin reddens as my fingers restrict her oxygen intake. She attempts to nod, but I squeeze harder, my cock hardening painfully, knowing her life is in my hands. Now isn't the right time to give in to my primal urges, but my body demands I take her. Releasing her throat, I unbutton my pants, shoving them down my thighs, along with my briefs. Her gown has ridden up past her hips, and I push her panties to the side, slipping my fingers through her arid slit. "So dry, little doll." Pushing two fingers into her mouth, she gags as I hit the back of her throat. "Suck."

She obeys, and I pull them from her mouth, shoving them into her dehydrated cunt. She winces, but I thrust my fingers in and out, her body betraying her, desire conquering the fear keeping her arousal at bay. Her hips begin to move as her pussy weeps, coating my fingers as I pull them free, driving my cock inside her until I bottom out, my pelvis grinding against her clit.

"Don't fight it, Olivia. You know you were made for me." I groan, her tight heat wrapping around me, begging for more.

She whimpers as I crash my mouth to hers, shoving my tongue past her lips, claiming what is mine. It takes her a few moments, but she kisses me back, giving her body what it craves.

Me.

No matter how angry or fearful she may be, she wants me. I'd love to see the inner workings of her mind when she tries to sort out that shit. The thought makes me grin, and I slam into her over and over, her low moans making my cock throb. "That's it, little doll. Come for me."

"No!" She sobs, turning her head to side, squeezing her eyes shut.

She's lost what's left of her fucking mind if she thinks she can deny me.

Picking up the pace, I pound into her, knowing she'll feel the aftereffects for days to come. Slipping my hand between our bodies, I pinch her clit, giving her no choice but to submit to me. "Come. Now."

She cries out, her body tensing beneath me, her tight cunt choking my cock like nothing I've ever felt. I groan against her lips, my own release ripping through me without warning, coating her inner walls with a ridiculous amount of cum.

My hips glide back and forth, our combined juices leaking out around my cock, and I bury my face in the crook of her neck, licking and suckling her salty skin. She trembles uncontrollably, her thighs loosely spread open instead of wrapped around my waist, her hands fisting the sheets rather than her arms wrapped around my neck.

She didn't call out my name or touch me the entire time. I frown. "You didn't enjoy yourself?"

She shakes her head, tears leaking from the corners of her eyes. "I didn't want this."

I choose to cup her cheek instead of giving into my rising irritation. "You were upset by what you saw earlier. Your body just needed a jumpstart. You want me as much as I want you, Olivia. But your mind is broken. That's why I'm here, little doll. To help you."

Her brows furrow, something flickering in her eyes I can't quite make out in the darkness. "I'm tired."

"I'll leave you to sleep." I sigh, letting my cock slip from her warmth. After straightening my clothes, I watch as she covers herself in silence, turning onto her side, giving me her back.

What the hell is wrong with her?

"I'll see you in a few hours," I say, but I'm met with more silence.

Opening the door, I leave her room, heading for my office.

CHAPTER FIFTEEN
OLIVIA

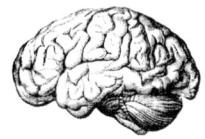

I'm dreading my session with *him* today.

After last night, or this morning, there's no sense of time in this place, I'm confused and hurt.

For the first time since I arrived in this hell, well over a month ago, I wish I could stay locked in this dark prison cell, alone. I'm losing myself piece by piece. Hell, the sedatives are becoming more appealing. At least I could sleep and escape this fucked up reality.

Atlas is cruel, and the longer I'm here, the more I realize just how sadistic he truly is. While my instincts scream to stay away from him, my heart can't ignore our time alone together.

Until last night.

As I fight to push away those memories, they assault my mind until they're clear as day.

The way he treats me in his office during those quiet

moments, I forget I'm in an asylum. The doctor/patient relationship becomes blurred while I'm in his arms. Every day I see him, just for a little while, I feel normal. I'll do anything to hang on to that.

If I could only stay in control and stop questioning him, I think we'll be okay.

The door opens to my room, Nurse Carter striding in. "Time to go, Miss Sterling."

Exhaling a shaky breath, I follow her quietly, completing my morning routine. I take my time, scrubbing the evidence of last night's fuck from between my thighs, a lone tear sliding down my cheek, mingling with the cool water spraying from the shower head. Shame slithers through me. He may have forced himself on me, but my body reacted, wanting his intrusion.

I came.

I didn't beg and plead for him to stop. I didn't push him away. I let him take what he wanted while my mind silently pleaded for it to be over.

Then I came.

I don't want to see him this morning, not after what he did to Mr. Henderson. What he did to me.

But I do care about him, and no matter how hard I try, I can't make those feelings go away.

He isn't my stepbrother.

He cares about me. He didn't want to hurt me last night; he just needed the connection. *Right?*

Once I'm dressed, I find Nurse Carter waiting for me outside the bathroom. She leads me to Atlas's office, and the door is already open. I step inside, closing it behind me, and take a seat on the couch.

He looks up from his computer, his face unreadable. "How are you feeling today, Olivia?"

As I meet his darkening gaze, all my worries from earlier fade away. "I'm okay."

He pushes his chair back, rising gracefully, circling the desk. He squats in front of me, taking my hands in his own. "Are you upset with me?"

My chest tightens. "Why did you do it?"

His brows furrow in confusion. "Do what?"

"Take me the way you did?" I grit out, heat spreading across the surface of my skin. He may care about me, but he doesn't get to use me and play dumb afterwards.

The back and forth in my mind is exhausting. Part of me wants to beat the shit out of him for what he did. But the other part likes that he wants me the way he does. Unapologetically.

Fuck, this place is making me crazier than I already was.

My fingers ache as his grip tightens around them. "I'll take you any way I want, any time I want. You belong to me, Olivia. I thought I made that clear the day you arrived."

My skin heats further, my breaths becoming shorter and quicker. Sweat beads across my hairline, my vision zeroing in on the set of his clenched jaw.

He's really a beautiful man, but all I can think about is ripping his fucking throat out. I continue staring as his lips tug into a smirk, his arrogance shining through like the sun's rays after a storm.

"There she is." He smiles widely. "Time for a new exercise in control." He releases my hands, taking the seat next to me. Unbuttoning his pants, he pushes them down his thighs along with his briefs, freeing his cock, and I lick my lips as it slaps against his abdomen. "Instead of fighting me, you're going to fuck me."

"What?" I snarl.

He fists my hair, pulling me until I'm straddling his lap. He leans in, his mouth too close to mine. "You're going to fuck me like you hate me, little doll."

My vision begins to dim at the edges, and I hyperfocus on his face. "I *do* fucking hate you."

He chuckles darkly. "Prove it."

My hands curl into fists as he lifts me up, positioning his cock at my entrance. A growl fills the room, and it takes a moment to realize it's coming from me. My back straightens, and I raise my arm, ready to knock him the fuck out when he drops me onto his cock, filling me so full it steals my breath, paralyzing me.

"Fuck!" He shouts, and if Nurse Carter is hanging around, I'm sure she heard him along with the torturous scream ripped from my throat.

"You motherfucker!" I sneer, slapping him across the face.

His entire body stiffens, his eyes snapping to mine. I don't know what the fuck he's thinking, but I don't have to wait long as his lips curve into a sadistic smile. "That's my girl. Let it out. Don't let it control you."

His words strike their mark, and the earlier signs of an episode slowly recede into the corners of my mind. He lifts my hips, thrusting up as he slams me down onto his big, beautiful cock. I bite my lip to muffle the moans threatening to escape from the heady mix of pain and pleasure. It's wreaking havoc on my body; my pussy craving his demented push and pull. My feelings for him border on wanting to kill him and never wanting this to end.

My core aches for him, my skin burns for him, but my mind wants to kill him.

He groans as I pin him to the couch, my hands on his chest. I find my rhythm, grinding my clit against him every time I drop my pussy onto his thick cock. My nails dig into the fabric of his shirt, and before I realize what I'm doing, I rip it open, buttons pinging off every surface around us.

He growls like the predator he is, and I rake my nails down his chest, mesmerized by the blood rising to the surface. He hums with satisfaction. "Fuck, little doll. Harder. This is what you need."

I grin, his skin gathering under my fingernails soothing

the violence I crave. "Let me guess. Your cock will cure my disorder?"

"There's my smart girl." He grins, his grip on my hips tightening, threatening bruises and tender skin for days.

His arrogance enrages me, and I raise my fist, punching him in the fucking eye. He grunts, his head whipping to the side, but his hips never stop moving. "No dick is that good, asshole."

His gaze snaps to mine, and before I can get a read on him, I'm on my back, my hands pinned above my head. "Let's test that theory." Gripping both my wrists in one of his hands, he raises the other, backhanding me across the face.

My body goes rigid, every cell of my anatomy focusing on the stinging pain. It spreads across my skin, igniting a rage so deep within me, it feels like I may implode. "I'm going to kill you." The words are low, and I don't recognize my own voice.

He leans in, brushing his lips across mine. I snap my teeth, and he chuckles. "You're not going to do a fucking thing except lay there and take what I give you like an obedient, little slut."

He rises to his knees, bringing my wrists to my stomach, pinning them in place. One of my legs is trapped between his body and the back of the couch. The other is hanging over his shoulder, and I curve it inwards, trying to kick him in the back of the head.

He slams into me, hitting my g-spot just right, and all the fight leaves my body. Using his grip on my wrists as leverage, he pistons into me over and over, and I lose all my senses. The bright light shining through the window disappears. The low hum of the electronics in his office fade away. I no longer feel the leather couch beneath me. The heavy weight on my chest dissipates, the throbbing in my head subsiding. The incessant need to slit his throat fades, as well as the voice encouraging me to do so.

There's nothing.

Only him.

His spicy scent surrounds me. The tight features of his face are all I see. The muscles of his chiseled body are all I feel. His short pants and deep groans are all I hear. He consumes me in every way, and I fucking hate him for it. "Atlas," I whimper.

His eyes widen a fraction before he falls on top of me, his forearms catching the brunt of his weight. "Olivia." He groans as if he's in pain. His eyes search my face before sliding his hands beneath my back, gripping my shoulders roughly. His thrusts deepen, hitting every secret place inside me I didn't know existed. "You'll never fucking escape me."

My core tightens at his words, something explosive coiling deep in my belly. He drives inside me as if he's possessed, and it's painful in a way that brings me pleasure beyond anything words can describe.

"Let go." I groan, and he does. My hands slide up his chest, trailing up his neck, sinking my fingers into his hair. Tugging roughly, his head snaps back, his hips thrusting faster, and deliciously harder.

He circles his hips, and I'm careening towards a wave of terrifyingly beautiful oblivion. He must sense it as my lips part, and he slams his palm over my mouth. A muffled scream tears through my throat, instantly raw from the force of it. My vision darkens as pleasure barrels through my limbs, a mixture of agony and bliss. My muscles clench so tightly, pricks of pain assault my nerves. The orgasm burns through me, hot and wild for long minutes before fading into flickering embers, my body feeling weightless and satiated.

In the distance, I sense his thrusts becoming erratic, a deep growl leaving his chest. His warm cum fills me so completely, it leaks out around him, sliding down my ass.

His hips come to a halt, and our gazes lock. Without breaking eye contact, he slides my leg from his shoulder, wrapping it around his waist. He frees my other leg to do the same, and he shifts, his forearms on either side of my head taking the brunt of his weight. "How do you feel?"

I blink. "I don't have the urge to kill you anymore, but I still don't like you."

"That's fair." He chuckles.

The death glare I send his way should cut off his amusement, but the bastard just smiles. Is this what my life will be? Having an infuriating doctor who I'll fuck constantly so I don't murder him? The thought has the walls closing in on me, and he must sense the shift. His body presses into me with more weight, and I'm unsure if it's for comfort, or he thinks I'm about to bolt.

"What?" He asks.

"I'm never getting out of here, am I?"

His jaw clenches as if I've offended him. "No one leaves Wellard Asylum."

CHAPTER SIXTEEN
ATLAS

Olivia sits on the couch across from my desk, staring blankly through the window.

She's been acting strangely since our therapy fuck a few days ago. She seems more withdrawn, her eyes vacant when I catch her gaze. While I enjoyed her tight cunt wrapped around my cock, she's acting as though she didn't enjoy the multiple orgasms she received.

Pushing my chair back from the desk, I clasp my hands behind my head, watching her quietly. As a psychiatrist, it's my job to find out what makes my patients tick, where their abnormal thoughts take them. But every time I think I have Olivia figured out; she shifts in a different direction. Luckily for her, I enjoy a challenge. It'd be a shame to grow bored of her. What would I do with my time?

My phone vibrates on the desk, and I know who the

private number belongs to. I answer quickly, heading into the bathroom, closing the door behind me. "Yeah."

"Do you have what I need?" Simon, the black market organ dealer snarls down the line.

Everything sold on the black market is dangerous territory, but selling organs is an entirely different ball game. These people are ruthless, and won't think twice about ending your life. They'll kill you when you least expect it, finding someone else to replace you before your body is cold. It's a criminal empire where the demand is high, and you're paid a ridiculous amount of money to uphold your end of the deal.

Fail and die.

That's the bottom line.

While I respect the clear rules, I thoroughly dislike Simon, and his shitty attitude. "I have a candidate. You know I have to be careful."

"We're on a clock, Stone. Don't fuck me over. I won't hesitate to put a bullet between your eyes."

"Don't threaten the man who supplies the organs, asshole. I'll call you before surgery so you can arrange the transport. Until then, fuck off." I end the call before he can respond.

I'll need to speed up the vetting process with Henderson. Trapping him in the Utica bed was all part of the testing I'm conducting. I needed him in a high stress situation to make sure the bastard's heart didn't give out. It's held strong so far. The final trials consist of administering multiple sedatives, ensuring his heart can withstand the medications. If it's successful, Mr. Henderson will be a silent hero, donating his vital organ to someone in need.

While it's heartwarming, and oh so touching, I'm more excited about the compensation I'll receive. The money will be added to the sizeable bank account I have, the cash solely for the purpose of early retirement. I'm still young. What's the point of working until I'm too old to spend the money I've saved? I want to live my life, and if Olivia is a good girl, I'll find a way for her to live it with me. As I open the bathroom door, Olivia is standing there, her eyes narrowed with suspicion.

The balls on this girl.

There's no sign of embarrassment even though she's been caught.

"Were you eavesdropping, little doll?" I ask, brushing past her.

She scoffs. "You're selling people's organs?"

My jaw clenches. "You shouldn't have heard that."

She watches me for a few moments before a grin tugs at her lips, followed by a surprisingly creepy cackle. My body goes rigid as she doubles over, laughing hysterically for several long minutes. She's gasping for air, tears leaking from her eyes while I'm growing more agitated. Opening the top drawer of my desk, I slip a sedative filled syringe into my pocket, just in case.

She finally composes herself, her gaze snapping to mine, heavy judgement in her eyes. "Everything about you is fucking disgusting. You're a psychopath masquerading as a doctor. And what's worse, you think you're actually helping people when in reality, you get off to the torture. You make me fucking sick."

Two strides, and I grip her biceps, pushing her against the wall. "Go on, little doll. Tell me how you really feel. Oh wait. It doesn't matter because you're fucking mine. I'll do whatever I want, whenever I want, and there's not a fucking thing you can do about it."

She spits in my face. "I hate you."

Wiping the expelled saliva from my eyes, I grin. "You only think you do now." She tenses at my words, her eyes tracking the movement as I pull the syringe from my pocket, removing the cap with my teeth. Turning my head to the side, I spit it out onto the floor. "You just wait."

She lands a blow to my jaw, but I recover quickly. Releasing her bicep, I wrap my fingers around her throat. She claws at my arm as I restrict her airway, but I'm stronger.

I'll always be stronger.

I sink the needle into her skin just above my fingers. The fight slowly leaves her body as the sedative takes hold, and she sinks to the floor. Blood oozes from the cuts and scrapes her nails left behind, and I lift my arm to my mouth, licking the warm liquid from my skin.

I wish it were hers.

Fucking hell, I admire her strong will, her fiery spirit. It makes my cock hard. I'd love nothing more than to fuck the attitude right out of her. Wake up every morning to see it's returned, just to fuck it out of her again. Shaking my head, I push the fantasy from the forefront of my mind. There's more pressing matters to attend to.

It's time to teach my little doll a lesson about sticking her nose where it doesn't belong.

CHAPTER SEVENTEEN
OLIVIA

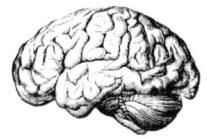

My eyes won't open, and I've become entirely too familiar with this feeling.

I've been drugged. *Again.*

Fucking Atlas.

He's such a piece of shit. I'll never understand how I couldn't see it at first. Why couldn't I see past the charm, the bullshit façade?

"Kill him!" The little voice whispers into my mind for the millionth time.

Believe me, bitch. If I could, I would.

My head is throbbing but when I try to move it, I can't. Attempting to lift my hands to my head, I can't move those either. Same for my legs. Warring with the pain shooting through my skull, I peel my eyes open, and I shudder. I'm sitting in front of a wall-length mirror. My head, arms, torso and legs are strapped into a wooden chair. It reminds me of the electric chairs I've seen on crime documentaries following death row inmates.

No. No. No.

This can't be fucking happening.

Just as I notice a door behind me, it opens. Atlas walks in with a sly grin on his face, and my stomach churns. "Hello, little doll," he coos, and the sound of his voice has bile rising in my throat.

I steel my spine and lift my chin the best I can while strapped to this fucking chair. "What form of torture will you be performing today, Dr. Stone?"

His grin widens to a full, beaming smile. "We're going to play a game."

He walks to the corner of the room, wheeling over a cart and stool I didn't see before. He sits in front of me, opening the second drawer of the cart. He pulls out a handful of long, skinny papers, laying them on top. He lifts one of the paper sleeves, slowly pulling an object from the packaging.

My body begins shaking uncontrollably.

Needles.

I watch in horror as he unwraps ten needles, carefully laying them in a row on top of a white cloth.

What the fuck is he going to do with those?

He picks one up, holding it in the space between us. "Today, you'll learn how to keep your mouth shut." He reaches for my hand, lifting my index finger as far as the restraints will allow.

No matter how hard I try, it won't curl into my fist. It must be the aftereffects of the sedative. I grit my teeth as he moves the needle closer to my fingertip.

The voice in my head is chanting now. "Kill him! Kill him! Kill him! Kill him!"

I'm strapped to a chair, a lunatic coming at me with a needle. What the fuck am I supposed to do? I begin fighting, pulling against the restraints, growling at the bastard as if it'll make him stop.

My skin pops and fire shoots through my hand as he slides the needle beneath my fingernail, sinking it deep into the nail bed. A scream tears from my throat, my muscles straining against the leather straps. My finger burns like it's being held within a flame, and I grit my teeth against the searing pain. My face begins to ache with how tightly my eyes are squeezed shut. I can't open them, even as he slides another needle into my middle finger.

One.

Two.

Three.

Four.

My senses focus on my jaw aching from grinding my teeth.

My throat raw from screaming through each pop of the skin on my fingertips.

My head throbbing from the sedatives and unleashed rage spearing through my veins.

Another needle pierces the nail bed of my ring finger, and everything disappears.

Silence.

No pain.

I'm floating in a void. Only the sound of my breathing filters through the darkness.

One. Breathe in.

Two. Breathe out.

Three. Breathe in.

Four. Breathe out.

My mind refuses to allow anything other than counting and breathing.

"Shhh." The voice whispers, and my mind shifts, the counting stops. *"Stay calm. I will get you through this."*

I startle. The little voice in my head usually only demands

death. It unleashes a part of me that would otherwise lay dormant. Hearing the soothing tone now throws me for a loop. It's abrupt presence always surfaces right before a rage episode occurs. I've always thought it was a side effect of my disorder, a unique way of protecting me. But now I wonder, is there someone else living inside my head? Do I have another personality acting as a defender, shielding me from the things I can't handle? My previous doctor told me he didn't believe I had multiple personalities. Something about my symptoms not meeting the criteria. Atlas hasn't mentioned it either.

"Calm." It whispers again, and I snap back to reality.

The sound of Atlas's harsh breathing reaches my ears. The cold dampness in the room assaults my skin. Adrenaline buzzes through my body, and I know what's about to happen.

My eyes snap open, and I meet the cold gaze of my tormentor. My abuser. My enemy.

I will take his life.

I'll beg the voice in my head to let me hang on to the memory. Let me be present and watch the life drain from his dark, emotionless eyes.

Glancing down at my hands, my gaze darts from one to the other, and I feel nothing as I see nine needles protruding from my fingertips. Our gazes collide once again, and for the first time ever, I see something resembling fear flash across his face. He's holding the final needle, gripping the thumb on my right hand. He blinks a few times before sinking it beneath my nail.

I don't flinch. I don't make a sound. I'm stoic, and his confused expression makes me break the silence and giggle. His brows furrow, which has me laughing harder, almost hysterically. He tilts his head to the side like a puppy trying to understand what he's looking at, and before I know it, I'm cackling so hard tears are steadily streaming down my cheeks.

"Little doll," he grits out, unimpressed by my reaction.

I don't respond, trying to catch my breath.

"Olivia," he growls.

Finally composing myself long enough to form words, I keep the smile on my face. "Did you enjoy making me your little pincushion?" His jaw clenches, but he doesn't respond. "What's the matter, Dr. Stone? Not the reaction you were hoping for?"

He lunges forward, wrapping his hand around my throat. "What the fuck is wrong with you?"

I laugh in his face. "I'm crazy, remember?"

He releases me, stepping back as if contemplating something. He leans down, plucking each needle from my fingers in quick succession, but I don't feel a thing. He grinds his teeth so violently, I expect to hear them shatter. He tosses the needles on the cart, returning his attention to me. "Alright, Miss Sterling. I'll show you how I treat crazy people."

CHAPTER EIGHTEEN
ATLAS

This bitch is testing me.

Her laughter sets me on edge, and I clench my fists to stop myself from doing something I'll regret.

I'd expected one of her episodes, not whatever the fuck this is. She appears completely lucid, in a cognitive state of mind. Based on her usual reactions to stress, and my own personal experience with her, it's as if another consciousness has come forward to shield her, but it's impossible.

Olivia doesn't have multiple personalities.

There are no notes mentioning symptoms in her file from Dr. Sweeney, nor have I witnessed this behavior from her before. I'm taken aback by the sudden change, and once we're finished here, I'll revisit my studies on multiple personality disorders to see if there may be a connection.

Although at this moment, I'm too pissed to care.

This type of therapy was designed to curb her attitude,

ensuring she doesn't open her mouth about what she over-heard. Instead, it seems to have unlocked another side of her completely.

Her intense stare is chilling, the hair on the back of my neck rising at the eerie atmosphere I find myself occupying. The expression is foreign on her beautiful face, and if I'm being honest with myself, it's quite bothersome. If I believed in religion, I'd say she's possessed by a demon. Some other-worldly creature hell-bent on staring me down until I vaporize or liquify.

I don't fucking like it.

Olivia has no control. I won't tolerate this bullshit game she's playing.

My irritation flares, and I pluck the needles from her fingertips in short intervals, gauging her reaction. She's smil-ing, yet her eyes are devoid of all emotion. Blood trickles from her fingertips, dark lines forming in the soft tissue of the nailbeds.

She's watching silently, that fucking grin on her face, unnerving me. I'm not used to this behavior from my patients, and I'm not in the habit of feeling a twinge of concern for my own safety. This is fucking madness, and I refuse to let her see how she's affecting me. My perficient skills allow me to mask my unease with a cocky smirk. "Alright, Miss Sterling. I'll show you how I treat crazy people."

Giving her my back, I stride over to the door, knocking three times. I retreat a few steps, and it opens a few seconds later. Nurse Carter enters, pushing a cart with the electrocon-vulsive machine. She's already wrapped the metal head piece with cloth, a bowl of water sitting beside it.

It's almost as if she knew this would be needed today.

I dip the muffs into the cool liquid, placing them on Olivia's temples, water trickling down the sides of her face.

She gives nothing away, her expression unbothered, almost bored. Surely, deep down inside, she's terrified.

That's what I tell myself because I don't have an answer otherwise.

As I take the mouthguard from the cart, she opens her mouth willingly, and I slide it inside.

Is she fucking with me?

No one can disassociate this well when threatened with so much pain.

Reaching for the machine, I flip the power switch, the hum of electricity roaring to life. Without hesitating, I press the button, raw power surging into her body. Her delicate limbs extend with tension, the cords in her neck straining against the agony she's experiencing. The vertical bands of muscle bulge as if they're going to explode from her throat as her body tries to bow, but the restraints keep her in place. The mouthguard thickens around the edges as her teeth clamp down so tightly, I have no doubt they'd shatter if they weren't protected.

The pure energy rockets through her system, and because she's been more defiant than usual, I allow the electricity to soak into her body a few seconds longer than last time. Her skin becomes ghostly pale, her eyes snapped shut so tightly, the vein in her forehead pulses. Or maybe that's from the electroshock. Chuckling to myself, my hand continues to hover over the switch that can end my little doll's misery.

A throat clears beside me, and I turn my head, reminded Nurse Carter is in the room. "Dr. Stone, I believe she's had enough."

Rage blurs my vision.

Who the fuck does she think she is?

"If I wanted your opinion, Nurse Carter, I'd ask for it. Leave the room, now." I point towards the door.

She hesitates for a moment, not leaving until I've flipped the switch, ensuring the power is turned off.

I really need to kill that cunt.

The door closes and I return my attention to Olivia. She lies motionless, the infuriating smile long gone and my chest loosens. Pressing two fingers to the side of her neck, her pulse is weak, but it's still there.

You took it too far.

Lifting her eyelids, I'm startled by what I find. Multiple blood vessels have ruptured; the whites of her eyes littered with crimson lines.

Fuck.

I'll have to do some research to see if she's going to heal on her own, or if she'll need to see an ophthalmologist. I have zero interest in trying to explain that to Halstead. He'd be more concerned about why I give a fuck if her vision is damaged. He'd soon let her suffer.

As I unbuckle the straps on the chair, she slumps forward, and I move quickly to catch her before she falls. She weighs nothing as I scoop her into my arms, carrying her out of the room, down the hall. Nurse Carter steps to the side as I pass, her eyes cast downward.

"Return the equipment and sanitize the chair," I say, realizing Olivia's backside is dripping with urine.

Entering my office, I lay her on the leather couch, making a mental note to sanitize it once she's returned to her room. Heading into the bathroom, I reach into the cabinet, pulling down a spare gown and panties. I've kept a few extra clothing items for her in case of an emergency. Grabbing a few cleansing wipes from the drawer, I make my way back to my office.

Kneeling at her side, I pull the soiled clothing from her body. It's awkward and her dead weight is inconvenient, but I make do. Spreading her legs open, I wipe the urine from her skin, ensuring she's clean before putting on the underwear. Pulling her into a seating position, I slip the gown over her head, letting it fall down her body.

I sit back on my heels, wondering what the next step will be. There's no telling what version of Olivia we'll be greeted with when she wakes up. Until we know for sure, I'll wrap her in a straitjacket. She's going to be unconscious for a while, she won't even know. I'll instruct Nurse Carter to keep an eye on her vitals and alert me when she wakes up.

While I may have pushed the boundaries today, one thing remains the same. Olivia needs to learn a lesson. If shock therapy and needles won't to the trick, I have no choice but to resort to deprivation therapy. I tried it on a small scale before, and it sent her into an episode the same day.

This time, I'm hoping it'll be the catalyst that'll finally shatter her mind. While I enjoy the challenge she presents, time is of the essence. My plan is constantly changing, adapting to her needs as they arise. I'm running out of options, and the time for games is over.

If Oliva doesn't break soon, I'll have to destroy her myself.

CHAPTER NINETEEN
OLIVIA

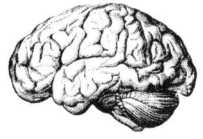

I woke up a few minutes ago, and I'm lying here, staring into the darkness.

My head is throbbing, but I try to piece things together. I've got nothing, no idea how long I've been out this time. I thought the bastard drugged me again when I tried to rub my eyes, and my arms wouldn't move. Slowly, I realized they were bound as I began fighting the tight space pinning my limbs.

He trapped me in a fucking straitjacket.

My temples ache and burn from the shock treatment. I don't remember much from the actual procedure, but my memories from the needles are still intact. While I may be actually insane, I can't help but think my mind is protecting me. It's keeping me from falling under Atlas's spell again. Shock therapy should've scrambled my brain, especially the way he does it, but I haven't lost myself this time.

I still fucking hate Atlas Stone.

He won't be able to make excuses this time. It was his decision to torture me. *His alone.*

The canvas material is harsh against my skin, unforgiving and suffocating. Panic bubbles up at the restriction, and I begin counting, trying to chase away the claustrophobia closing in on me.

One. Breathe in.

Two. Breathe out.

Three. Stay calm.

Four. I'm okay.

Repeating it over and over, I tap my toes on the cot mattress, concentrating on the numbers and rhythm until I fall asleep hours later.

When I open my eyes, it feels like I've been asleep for days. I notice immediately the straitjacket is gone. I'm not sure how they removed it without waking me, but judging by the way I feel, I'm positive they sedated me while I was asleep.

Strange.

With sedatives, I always wake up in a rage, but not the past couple of times. Something has changed, and it frightens me because I don't know if it's a good thing or bad. Am I getting better? Or has the disorder progressed? Chances are, I'll never find out. Atlas doesn't give a fuck, and I'm sure the other doctors here are the same. I'm on my own, with no way to find answers.

I push myself up from the bed, leaning back against the cold, concrete wall. It takes a few moments for my eyes to focus, but when they do, I'm surprised the slot on my door is open, a stream of light shining into the dark, damp cell. That flicker of joy is short lived as I look around the area.

A bucket sits in the corner of the room, a roll of toilet paper on the ground beside it. Small pieces of the tissue are scattered across the floor, surrounded by rat droppings.

I guess Gus wanted to play.

My nose scrunches at the thought of using the contaminated tissue to wipe myself, but I'm distracted as a foul smell assaults my nostrils. Wetness registers against my skin, and my head hangs as I realize I've pissed the bed.

How long have I been knocked out?

A hint of body odor hits me next, and I cringe. I feel like a fucking caged animal, unbathed, using the bathroom where it lays.

Tears threaten to fall, but I grit my teeth, the action sending sharp pains through my jaw, shooting up to my sensitive temples. Gently as possible, I prod the areas where he put the metal thing on my head, sending shockwaves of electricity through my brain. The skin is crusty and tender, but I'm grateful I don't remember the pain. My body is sore, and I know it's from my limbs tensing throughout the ordeal. My jaw is killing me, and I open my mouth, working it back and forth. It doesn't help, and I sigh, feeling hopeless and defeated.

I'm in hell.

Literal fucking hell, and my doctor is Lucifer in the flesh.

A shadow snuffs out the light before a bowl and a plastic cup are shoved through the opening in the door. I jump from the bed, my legs trembling, dizziness assaulting me as I rush to stop them. "Excuse me!"

The orderly turns back, but he doesn't speak.

"Can you tell Nurse Carter I need to speak with her?"

The slot closes, and I'm forced into darkness, wondering if he'll deliver the message. I feel around, taking the bowl and cup, heading towards the bed. Avoiding the urine stain, I cross my legs, leaning back against the wall, staring into the void as I gulp down the water. My stomach burns with hunger as I dip my finger into the bowl, bringing a scoop of slop to my lips. My throat constricts as I gag around the texture, holding my breath to avoid the taste. Breathing through my nose as I swallow, it's absolutely fucking disgusting, but without it I'll starve.

That doesn't seem so bad.

Intrusive thoughts brush the corners of my mind, and I shake my head, refusing to entertain them.

I won't give up. *Not yet.* I'm not sure why the hell I'm clinging onto this existence, but there has to be more to life than this.

The metal slot in the door flies open, startling me. "What is it, Miss Sterling?"

I'm rooted to the spot, making no attempt to move. "I'd like to take a shower and use a toilet."

"Your bathroom privileges have been revoked, including showers. You are to stay in your room until further instructions are given by Dr. Stone."

My chest caves in at her words.

I'm nothing more than an animal.

When I don't reply, the clicking of her heels alerts me she's walked away. She left the slot open, and I'm thankful the stream of light has returned. Before I get lost in my head again, a squeaking noise comes from below, and tears prick my eyes.

Gus.

I chug the rest of the water before lying down on the edge of the bed. I can't stomach any more of the shit food, so I slowly place the bowl on the floor, leaving my arm dangling over the side of the mattress.

"Hi, buddy. I've missed you."

He hesitates for a few moments before moving closer, his nose twitching.

"You can have it, Gus Gus. Come on, cutie pie."

He reaches the bowl, standing up on his hind legs to look over the rim. He looks up at me, and I smile. Gently, I flip the bowl over, emptying the food onto the floor. He dives in. Taking a chance, I hover my index finger above him, slowly moving closer to pet his dark, gray fur. He jumps back, but the lure of food brings him forward again. "I'll never hurt you, Gus. You're my friend." I rest my finger on his back, softly running it down the length of his spine. He tenses, looking up at me. "You're my only friend."

He resumes eating, and I continue stroking his back, adding another finger every few minutes until I'm petting him with my palm. "Do me a favor, buddy. Don't shred the toilet paper, okay?" He allows me to caress his slick fur, whether he's too hungry to care, or he senses my emotions.

Once the food is gone, he tilts his head up. "Is your tummy full? Come back any time you want, sweet boy. If I have food when you visit, it's yours." He sniffs my hand, and I pet him one last time before he waddles away with a swollen belly.

I may be no one, but maybe Gus is happy to have me around.

I don't want to think about how much time has passed while I'm locked in this cell twenty-four hours a day.

I'm sleeping in dried urine, and I couldn't allow myself to have another accident. Heavy with shame, I've forced myself to use the bucket in the corner. The thought of using the cont-aminated toilet paper made me nauseous, but does it really matter at this point? Maybe I'll get an infection that'll speed up my journey to the afterlife.

The latch on the door clicks, startling me. Atlas strides in, oozing confidence, without a care in the world. "Hello, Olivia."

My gaze finds the metal bucket in the corner full of urine. The only silver lining is I haven't eaten enough to defecate in it. My skin prickles, his stare boring into the side of my face.

"You're too beautiful to be so filthy."

I refuse to look at him, to give him one ounce of my attention.

"You will bow to me, Olivia. I own you, and the faster you realize it, the better off you'll be."

My fingers flex as he comes closer, the movement pulling the skin tightly around my nails. Little sparks of pain spread through my fingertips, and I flinch.

He stops at the edge of the cot, towering over me. "You've soiled your bed, little doll." He chuckles, and if ever I wished for my rage to appear, it's now. He's the fucking devil, torturing his patients until he kills them, selling their organs on the black market.

Sick fuck.

Lifting my chin, my eyes lock onto his. I convey every ounce of hate and disgust I feel into my gaze. His brows furrow, and he takes a step back. He watches me for a few moments before schooling his features, his casual demeanor returning. Glancing at the bucket in the corner, his eyes dart back to me before heading for the door. "You smell atrocious. I'll send Nurse Carter in to take you to shower." He exits the room quickly and I smile.

If my own smell didn't turn my stomach, and my skin didn't itch constantly from the filth, I'd refuse the shower just to piss him the fuck off.

CHAPTER TWENTY
ATLAS

What I'm doing isn't working.

She has to be the most stubborn patient I've ever treated. Her strong will was admirable in the beginning but now I find it fucking infuriating. Why the hell does she have to be so difficult? Everything I've done is to help her be a better version of herself.

She consumes my every waking thought. I dream about her every night. I'm constantly revising my plan to get her out of here so we can have a life together. What else does she want from me?

The shock therapy didn't work as I'd hoped. The first treatment caused her mid-level memory loss, but it could've been a combination of the procedure and her episode occurring at the same time. The latest therapy session wasn't accompanied by a rage fit. That has to be the difference. It's the only conclusion my mind will accept.

She's been in complete isolation for a week.

She wore a straitjacket.

She lost the convenience of tending to her basic human needs.

She was provided with food and water, but just by looking at her, I could tell she hasn't been eating. She's pale, her cheekbones pronounced from malnutrition. It pained me to see her so filthy, sleeping in her own urine, but it had to be done.

She must be broken.

My efforts so far have not provided the desired results, but I refuse to lose hope.

I won't give up on her.

I haven't laid eyes on my little doll since I visited her room two days ago.

The space was needed to conjure a new plan. I must say, I'm excited about the scheme I've devised. I'm hardly capable of containing myself, imagining the hope in her eyes, the gratitude she'll feel, welcoming me back into her good graces.

It's risky, and it could go horribly wrong at any moment, but I'm willing to take the chance. If successful, it could change *everything*. I only need to sell it to Olivia, and hope she plays her part flawlessly.

CHAPTER TWENTY-ONE
OLIVIA

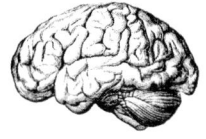

Nurse Carter brought me into Atlas's office about a half hour ago.

He wasn't here when I walked in, so I took the opportunity to sit in his chair, snooping through his drawers. It's not like anyone would care if I found something incriminating, but I looked through his shit regardless.

He's good.

There's no evidence of him torturing patients or selling their organs on the black market. He's an evil son-of-a-bitch, and he's untouchable. He can do whatever he wants, whenever he wants, to whoever he wants, and no one will say a fucking word. Just as I'm closing the last drawer, the door opens. Atlas saunters in, his arrogance so thick and suffocating, it pushes the oxygen from the room.

"Find anything interesting, little doll?"

"No. You keep your sins hidden well." I roll my eyes, standing from the chair.

As I round the desk, he blocks me. "Sins are overrated, don't you think? I live my life how I see fit. No higher power in the sky scaring me into living a certain way."

I shoulder check him as I pass, taking my usual seat on the couch. "You're a fucking monster no matter what you believe."

He sighs, running his hand through his hair. My eyes dart to the floor, refusing to look at him any longer. *How can someone so beautiful on the outside be so fucking rotten on the inside?*

He rolls his desk chair in front of me, sitting so close, our knees brush. "You'll forgive me one day, Olivia. Everything I've done was to help you. Can't you see that?"

Counting the blemishes on the floor, I answer distractedly. "Whatever helps you sleep at night, Dr. Stone."

Minutes of silence pass between us as I continue counting the scuffs and lines marring the floor. I count them multiple times until they equal an even number. My eyes find a poster on the wall behind his desk. I read each word slowly, counting the letters. If they equal an odd number, I combine the words until the letters equal an even number.

His next words have my eyes snapping to his. "I've talked to Dr. Halstead about having you released."

My mouth falls open, the breath whooshing from my lungs. "What?"

He smirks. "You belong to me, little doll. I won't have you locked in here any longer. You've made great progress with your disorders, and we'll continue outpatient treatment."

My head spins with all the possibilities of living a normal life.

A future.

But it all comes crashing down as I realize he'll still be a part of my life. My mouth closes, the oxygen returning to my lungs. "You said no one leaves here."

He nods. "No one has ever been legitimately released. We've had a few patients escape."

"Were they caught?"

"Some were. Some weren't."

"Oh." An escape plan never crossed my mind considering I'm in the isolation ward, locked in a concrete cell.

"I've spoken to him multiple times about you, and how you're a special case. You have a chance to be free, Olivia. I only need you to follow my instructions."

"Which are?" I ask, a pit forming in my stomach.

Dread.

It feels like I'm selling my soul to the devil.

He sits back in his chair. "We'll rehearse what you'll say. Do not stray from the script I provide, or he'll see right through it, and you'll never see the light of day again."

"What do I have to say?" My hands tremble, nausea churning in my belly.

He pats me on the knee, grinning. "We'll begin tomorrow."

Atlas Stone will either be my undoing, or the gateway to a new beginning.

You'd think I'd have hope, something to look forward to, but I'm not naïve enough to believe the latter.

CHAPTER TWENTY-TWO
ATLAS

P oor, little doll.
   When I gave her the news three days ago, I
   thought I'd see a glimmer of hope in her eyes, but
there was nothing.

She doesn't trust me.

While I've given her multiple reasons to hate me, she refuses to see I'm doing all of this for us. Our future. Together.

She's sitting on the couch, her hands in her lap, staring out of the window. She's showing no signs of distress or anger. It's odd to see her like this. My head tilts to the side as I watch her closely.

She's disassociated.

Damnit. We can't have that.

Striding over to the sofa, I take the seat next to her, and

I'm surprised she doesn't flinch away from my touch as I take her hand in mine. "Olivia, talk to me."

She continues gazing outside. "I'm fine. Just going over everything in my head." She pulls her hand from mine.

Irritation flares in my chest, but I push it down. She has no idea what's about to happen, and the part that brings me the most joy is the fact she won't remember a thing.

"Thank you for seeing us, Dr. Halstead," I say as we step into his office, sitting in the two seats in front of his desk.

He glances up from his paperwork, dropping his pen onto the wooden desktop. "Let's hear it, Stone."

I strongly dislike this old bastard, and while I'd like to pierce his jugular with his own pen, he has a part to play today. "As I informed you the last time we met, Miss Sterling has made wonderful progress in controlling her disorders. I feel she's ready to be released back into society with continued outpatient care, which I will provide."

Olivia sits beside me, stoic as a statue. I wish she would show some enthusiasm, or hopefulness, if only for my benefit. It really doesn't matter how she acts, or if she fucks up the speech we rehearsed. How this meeting ends is my only concern.

Dr. Halstead turns his head, meeting Olivia's gaze. Something feral rises up inside me at the way he assesses her. My hands clench into fists in my lap as I try to suppress the urge to leap over the desk and rip his fucking head off. Or I could tackle him to the floor, my expensive dress shoe caving his face in until he's unrecognizable. I could take the prize scalpel he keeps on his desk like a trophy, and slice open his-

"Do you have anything you'd like to say while you have my time, Miss Sterling?" Dr. Halstead's words interrupt my murderous thoughts.

Olivia meets his eyes. "Thank you for your time, Dr. Halstead. My mental illnesses have caused me to take a path I never imagined traveling down. I killed my father, step-mother, and stepbrother. While their deaths were brought on by physical and sexual abuse, I wish the outcome could've been different. I've also killed an orderly and attacked Dr. Stone while suffering from rage episodes." She pauses, and pride swells in my chest as she speaks with a steady voice. "Dr. Stone has performed shock therapy, as well as other methods to help in suppressing these episodes, so I can re-enter society as a wholly functional member."

Dr. Halstead leans back in his chair, folding his hands in his lap. "Thank you for your obviously scripted explanation, Miss Sterling. While I do appreciate your effort, I don't have the time nor the interest for a pathetic plea to leave Wellard Asylum. You're here for a reason. You're a murderer."

Olivia flinches away from his words like he slapped her across the face. I sit back in my chair, waiting for the show to begin. Lifting my hand to cover my mouth, I attempt to hide the grin tugging at my lips.

"After this little stunt, I'll instruct Dr. Stone to proceed with more frequent electroconvulsive therapy sessions. You're sick, and it's obvious our efforts up to this point have not rehabilitated you at all. No worries, Miss Sterling. We'll cast these demons from you one way or another." He picks up his pen, returning to his paperwork as if he didn't just shatter her world.

We're dismissed.

My eyes dart to Olivia, and excitement thrums through my veins as I watch the anger cover her pale skin with a heated flush. I don't know what she's been doing to suppress it these past few weeks, but how she looks now, it's come back with a fucking vengeance. My cock strains against my slacks, the anticipation of what's to come almost too much contain.

"You're not releasing me?" She asks, her voice low and controlled, and my heart rate picks up, preparing for her wrath.

He glances up with disdain. "No, Miss Sterling. You will not leave Wellard Asylum." His lips pull up in a sneer as he swings his gaze to me. "You may need to assess her learning comprehension skills as well, Dr. Stone. She seems a little slow."

And here we go.

Olivia shoots up from the chair, snatching the heavy name plate from Halstead's desk. She lunges forward, bashing him in the side of the head with it. His entire body snaps to the side, the chair flipping over, dumping him onto the floor. She launches herself over his desk, pouncing on top of him while he cradles his bleeding head.

I have a front row view of Olivia's beautiful rage, her unnatural strength, and her perfect ability to commit violence in a way that leaves you speechless. While I'd love to sit back, and watch her do this all afternoon, there's a plan that needs to be set in motion.

I have a part to play as well.

Rounding the desk, I feign concern for Halstead, attempting to stop Olivia from further attacking him. "Olivia, stop!" I shout, adding a terrified tremble to my voice.

I grip her biceps, pulling her from his body, wrapping my arms around her middle. Her back is to my chest as she flails so violently, I can barely keep her in my grip. She's screaming, clawing at my arms, but I hold on tightly as Halstead stands on shaky legs.

"You little bitch!" He roars.

I'm tempted to let her go so she can finish him off, but that outcome is not favorable for us.

"Fuck you! Fuck you! Fuck you! Fuck you!" She chants in a shrill voice, and I see what he's about to do before he does it.

Dr. Halstead is a no-nonsense kind of man. While he enjoys torturing patients, he'll dispose of them rather than deal with any minor inconveniences they may cause. He's gotten away with it for years because no one ever comes looking for them. They're abandoned, forgotten, never to be thought about again.

He grabs the scalpel from his desk, and in a move so fast I would've missed it if I blinked, he sinks the blade into Olivia's stomach.

For some reason, her wound causes my chest to tighten, and when her knees buckle, I fall to the floor with her. Placing my hand on the side of her head, I protect it from hitting the floor. Immediately, I reach into my pocket, pulling out the syringe while Halstead is fuming, pacing back and forth like a rabid animal.

Popping off the cap, I plunge the needle into her skin, and within moments, her breathing slows to a rate so shallow, it looks as if she's not breathing at all. The wound in her stomach is bleeding, but I'm certain he didn't hit any major organs. The old bastard is blind as a bat, and lucky for Olivia, it doesn't appear he hit anything vital. Slowly, I stand, ready to begin the second act.

"She's dying," I say, keeping my voice indifferent.

"No, she's not. I didn't hit any organs." He argues.

"Her breathing is labored. Her pulse is too slow. She's fading fast. You hit an organ, but I can't tell which one with all the blood." I lie, knowing I need to get her out of here. "What do you want me to do? Save her or get rid of her?"

He stands frozen, watching her chest before responding. "Damnit. She's an issue, Stone. Get rid of her."

I nod. "Consider it done."

"Not a trace," he snarls, running his hands down his face.

I ignore him as I bend down, scooping Olivia into my arms. He opens the door as I carry her from the office, and once I hear it close behind me, I grin.

Checkmate.

Only one thing left to do.

CHAPTER TWENTY-THREE
ATLAS

The drive home is quiet.

I expected Olivia to be awake by now, but I haven't heard any banging from the trunk of my car.

My fingers tap against the steering wheel, my body buzzing with anticipation as I make the long journey to my home. Is this how children feel when they open presents on Christmas morning? I wouldn't know. I didn't care about any of that shit when I was younger. My interests were centered around dissecting animals and avoiding my apathetic parents.

Pulling into the driveway, I park the car and pop the trunk, revealing Olivia's unconscious body as I round the back of the vehicle. I cleaned and stitched the wound in her abdomen inside my office before we left the asylum. She's remained knocked out longer than I anticipated, the mental exhaustion and her injury finally taking its toll.

Scooping her into my arms, I take her inside the house, heading for the spare bedroom. She stirs in my hold, her warm breath caressing the side of my neck. My cock hardens, desperate to be inside her fragile, undernourished body.

Stay focused, Stone.

Carrying her into the room I've prepared, I lay her on the bed, carefully removing the blood-stained gown from her body. She's truly beautiful with her red hair and pale skin, reminiscent of a sun goddess hidden away in the darkness for too long. My gaze travels her body, a groan slipping from my lips as I admire her nude form. Needing a distraction, I buckle the leather restraints around her wrists and ankles, leaving her spread eagle in the bed.

My cock aches at the sight of her, and I unbutton my pants, pushing them down my thighs, instant relief hitting me as my length springs free. My fingers wrap around my shaft, squeezing the base to ease the throbbing. Standing at the edge of the bed, I stare at her parted lips, stroking myself with a firm grip. My gaze travels down her body, and I pump myself harder, faster, the sensation almost too much by the time my eyes lock onto her pretty, pink cunt.

I think of how she felt around me, squeezing me, and my hand mimics the memories. My pleasure is building, but something is missing. *I need more.*

Kicking off my shoes, I rid myself of my pants and briefs, climbing onto the bed, straddling her face. Those dry, plump lips are begging to be stretched, and while she won't be an active participant in achieving my release, I know the simple feel of her around me will do the trick.

Gripping my cock, I slide it into her mouth, not stopping until the head hits the back of her throat. I suppress a groan as her warmth envelopes me, her limp tongue gliding along the underside of my shaft. Pulling out to the tip, I plunge back inside, harder, deeper. She whimpers but remains uncon-scious, and I continue abusing her slender throat, chasing the high only she can provide. After a few more pumps, my cock swells, and I abruptly pull out, painting her beautiful face with my cum. Pleasure rolls through my entire body, the force of it so powerful, I lunge forward, bracing myself on the headboard. It takes me a few moments to recover, and I grin as I look down at my little doll.

Bringing my hand to her cheek, I gather some cum with my fingers, running it through her hair. Once I'm satisfied, I rub the rest of it into her skin, spreading it across her face, down her neck, across her breasts. Her ghostly complexion shimmers, and I bend down, trailing my tongue across her lips.

Fucking delicious.

My cock jumps in response, hardening fully once again.

I'll never get enough of her.

My fingers glide down the valley between her breasts, her abdomen, over her pronounced hip bone. They have a mind of their own as they slip between her thighs, spreading her pussy lips open. I lick my lips, suddenly starving for Olivia's sweet, unique flavor. Crawling down her body, I press my face to her core, my tongue darting out, licking her from ass to clit.

Fuck.

Sucking her clit into my mouth, I slide two fingers inside her opening, thrusting in and out slowly. After a few minutes, her pussy begins to weep, the sound of her arousal filling the air around us. My control snaps, and I move over her, lining my cock up with her entrance. My hips snap forward, driving inside her so forcefully, her ankles strain against her bindings.

"Fuck, little doll. If only you were awake to scream my name." I groan against her throat, nipping the side of her neck.

My mind loses all rational thinking skills, and I fuck her

into the mattress as if my life depends on it. I give no thought for her comfort, or how sore she'll be when she wakes up. In this moment, she solely exists for my pleasure, a silent fuck doll, none the wiser to the brutal assault on her body.

My release creeps down my spine, my cock swelling right before I erupt inside her swollen cunt. Cum fills her tight, little hole, leaking out around me as I continue driving inside her until I'm satisfied. Her name is ripped from my lips as my body collapses, my chest heaving while struggling to regain my senses.

Rolling onto my side, I lay my head on her chest, listening to the steady rhythm of her heartbeat. My hand cups her pussy tightly, sealing her entrance so my cum stays inside her.

My mind wonders, and I find myself thinking of the future.

If I were capable of love.

If there is one person in this world who deserves it.

It would be her.

My perfect, little doll.

We've been at my home for a week now. I've put in for a few weeks of vacation time to spend with Olivia. It's not off to a great start.

She woke up three days ago, and it was anticlimactic to say the least.

While the stab wound is healing nicely, no sign of infection, she hasn't spoken a word.

She refuses to look at me.

I've never been treated like this before, and I highly disapprove. She's acting like I don't exist, like I'm not the one nursing her back to health, feeding her, giving her sponge baths.

Ungrateful fucking brat.

If she's well enough to have a shitty attitude, then she's well enough for the next step.

Hold onto your rage as long as you can, little doll.

It's all about to disappear.

CHAPTER TWENTY-FOUR
ATLAS

A couple of years ago, Dr. Halstead introduced me to the *lobotomy*.

Fascinated by the inner workings of the mind, I found myself consumed by the idea of rewiring someone's brain. I spent the majority of my time researching the history of the procedure and learning how the process has evolved. We were only taught a fraction about lobotomies in my college courses; it was skimmed over because it's seen as taboo.

The original leucotomy, also known as the prefrontal lobotomy, provided me with a glimpse into the technique, consisting of drilling a hole into the side or top of the patient's skull, exposing their frontal lobe. That alone has my interest piqued, and I couldn't stop myself from digging deeper. The doctor used a scalpel to cut the nerve fibers, the idea being to force the brain to develop new neural pathways, hoping for better emotional responses. While anesthesia was given to numb the brain, the patient was awake, and often asked to recite poetry while the procedure was being performed.

Some people thought it was barbaric, but I found it intriguing.

Another doctor tried a variation of the leucotomy. Instead of cleaving the nerves with a scalpel, he used a tool called a leucotome with a narrow shaft much like a syringe. It housed a wire that was inserted into the brain, severing the connections by rotating to core out brain tissue.

I found this alternative creative, but nothing compares to the *transorbital lobotomy.*

Most people refer to it as the *icepick lobotomy.*

The doctor who evolved the procedure from drilling a hole into someone's skull to simply piercing their eye socket was a man to be admired. The public disgraced him, labeling him as a narcissist instead of the genius he actually was. The man had no formal surgical training, yet he performed thousands of lobotomies on people who suffered from different types of mental illness. He refined the lobotomy, making it possible for psychiatrists such as myself to execute the treatment in office, without a hospital stay. His method provided a faster recovery time, the swelling in the brain decreased by weeks.

He literally pulled an icepick from his kitchen drawer, and used an actual hammer to perform the first transorbital lobotomy. He said the other doctor's unsuccessful attempts were due to unsturdy instruments.

The man had balls of steel, I'll give him that.

They later named the icepick an orbitoclast, and people were standing in line to have their brains *rewired.* The articles about his work were insane.

Pun intended.

He used shock therapy to render his patients unconscious.

He'd peel back their eyelid, inserting the icepick into the orbital socket, giving it a few taps with the hammer to break through the bone plate, and wiggle the icepick around to sever the frontal lobe. A towel would be held beneath their mouth and nose to catch mucus leaking from their orifices.

It was incredible.

I'd give anything to have been around back then, to witness the procedure in person.

An answer to mental illness was uncovered, but as usual, all good things must come to an end. The public got wind of some unpleasant side effects and a few deaths. All hell broke loose, and the doctor was banned from performing any more lobotomies. Convulsions, confusion, partial paralysis, and zombie-like behavior were reported, but with all experimental treatments, there'll always be failures. It's part of the process.

After brain hemorrhaging, trouble speaking, and loss of personality were brought to the attention of the medical boards, lobotomies were forbidden, and slowly faded from existence. Some doctors still practice the treatment under the radar, and lucky for me, Dr. Halstead is one of them.

They portrayed the doctor as a monster, deeming himself as a god, his ego too large to see the scope of what he was doing. I see him as an artist, an innovative thinker, a unique man who challenged nature. He may have been crucified in the public eye, but I think highly of his abilities, and I'm beyond grateful to follow in his footsteps.

This will change everything.

While I've never performed a lobotomy myself, I've watched and learned while Dr. Halstead has on multiple occasions. The anticipation pumping through my veins has it's own pulse inside my head. I've never felt so alive. I couldn't wait any longer, and I gave Olivia something to help her sleep soundly, instead of sedating her. The familiarity of restraining her brings a smile to my face.

Soon, little doll.

Once she wakes up, she'll be mine forever without question. She'll have no choice but to look to me for guidance and answers. I'll be her hero. Her savior.

Nothing will come between us.

She'll never be overwhelmed by her disorders again, and I'll have my beautiful, little plaything at my disposal whenever I want. As soon as Olivia opens her emerald eyes, she'll be at my mercy, more so than before. While I'm confident she's healed enough to have the lobotomy, I've given her a valium to calm her nerves and mind. The last thing I need is her fighting me during this delicate procedure.

As I sit beside her, watching her sleep peacefully, she begins to stir, and the excitement is like a kickstart to my chest. Her beautiful eyes flutter open, a cold stare pinning me with hatred.

I'll be glad when that look is gone.

"What are you going to do to me now?" It's the first words she's spoken since I've brought her here, and I must say, it adds a little pep to my step.

Confirming the strap around her head is secure, my thumb wipes away the lone tear leaking from the corner of her eye. "I'm going to fix you, little doll."

Her eyes fall shut as she whispers, "I just want to be free."

"I'm going to free your mind, Olivia. It'll all be over soon." Tracing her left eyebrow with my fingers, I grin, knowing my words are true. "Now open your eyes."

Her gaze finds mine, and so many emotions flash across her face.

Worry.

Terror.

Defeat.

She's yet to realize she's being given a gift, not understanding how truly lucky she is to have met me. I'm going to banish the demons from her mind, and give her the opportunity for a real life.

With me.

"The medication I gave you has had time to take effect. Let's begin." She blinks in response. "Would you like me to talk you through it, little doll?" I ask, putting on a pair of latex gloves.

"No," she whispers so softly, I almost miss it.

This is it.

I'm about to change both our lives.

"Look down," I tell her.

She does as I ask without hesitation. Lifting a cotton swab from the metal tray, I dip it into a small bowl of water. Once it's soaked through, I lift it to her eye, carefully pinching her eyelashes, rolling the eyelid over the cotton swab. Removing the applicator, the eyelid stays in place.

Gripping the orbitoclast between my fingers, I lift it to her eye, and I'm surprised she doesn't flinch.

The valium is working well.

Or she's disassociated.

She won't be doing that anymore once I'm finished with her.

Pinching her eyelid, I pull it from the socket, flicking the cotton piece out of the way. Lifting the orbitoclast, I push it beneath her lid, running parallel with her nose until I feel resistance from the orbital plate.

The goal is to sever the nerve pathways in the frontal lobes of the brain, as well as severing the connections between the frontal lobes and the thalamus. The thalamus is part of the limbic system, which controls emotions, memories, and learning. These are all skills Olivia struggles with.

Sweat forms above my brows as I carefully lower her eyelid onto the metal of the ice pick. With my free hand, I reach for the hammer, taking a deep breath before gently tapping it through the orbital socket. The soft crack of bone dissolving under the light force of the mallet has me grinning.

Fucking incredible.

After penetrating the barrier, the orbitoclast slides into the frontal lobe, gliding smoothly into the brain.

I'm a medical professional, with fluent knowledge in all medical jargon, but there's only one way to describe the texture of the human brain.

Squishy.

A sharp inhale disrupts my thoughts. Daring a glance at her, Olivia's eyes have glazed over, disassociating herself from the situation entirely. While I don't blame her, I wish she'd show more interest in this complex yet monumental procedure. Dr. Halstead wasn't successful in his attempts, but my knowledge well surpasses his, along with my skills. He performed lobotomies as experiments. I'm doing this to benefit my patient, as well as myself.

Blood oozes from beneath her eyelid, gathering at the corner of the socket, trailing down her nose. Crimson merges with the clear mucus seeping from her nostrils, and I grab a gauze pad, wiping away the thick stream of fluid. I'm not concerned; some bleeding is to be expected. Placing the hammer back onto the metal tray, I reach for another gauze, soaking up the saliva leaking from the corners of her mouth with my free hand, discarding it onto the tray.

As I push further into the frontal lobe, I twist the orbitoclast slowly in a back-and-forth motion. A strangled sound leaves her throat, and my eyes fly to her. Gaze still glazed over, staring at the ceiling, her face is blank. The need to say something makes my throat itch, but even I'm not that kind of monster. I'll leave her in whatever world she's in right now.

Rotating the orbitoclast, I visualize Dr. Halstead's lobotomies. Mimicking his movements, I imagine the connections in her mind, the tool between my fingers cutting the links. If the lobotomy doesn't work as it should, I'll have to assess the aftereffects before deciding her fate. If her symptoms aren't a burden, I'll figure out a way to make things work. If the side effects *are* too much to manage, I'll be merciful by putting her out of her misery. While she belongs to me, and I'd prefer to have her in my life, I won't support her in a vegetative state.

It's cruel to keep her that way.

That line of thinking is pointless anyway. I'm confident in my abilities. My skills are perfection, and I know she'll come out of this better than she was before.

And it'll be because of me.

Slowly, I retract the tool from her brain, easing it out of her eye socket. A trail of blood trickles from the wound as I drop the orbitoclast onto the metal tray. She doesn't flinch at the clanking sound, and it's all the confirmation I need.

I've missed wearing belts.

Reaching for a towel, I wipe the blood and mucus from her face. "Can you hear me, little doll?"

She blinks once, but she doesn't speak. I begin unfastening the restraints on her wrists when I notice a puddle of liquid on the table. She may be the object of my obsession, but her weak bladder is quite annoying.

Scooping her into my arms, I take her into the bathroom to clean her up. She's dead weight as I wrestle to remove her soiled gown, wiping away the urine from her skin with a cloth. Once I'm finished, I carry her into the bedroom she'll be staying in, placing her on the bed.

She's catatonic, her eyes open but unseeing. I wonder where she is right now.

The swelling in her brain should be minimal, but when she wakes from her current state, she'll likely have a migraine, and a black eye. I'll check her temperature every few hours to ensure she doesn't have a fever. She lies motionless as I cover her body with the blanket, flipping off the lamp on the nightstand, quietly leaving the room.

Heading for the shower, I undress, stepping under the

warm spray. Mentally replaying the procedure, pride swells in my chest, realizing I've done something miraculous. I've penetrated Olivia's brain with expert precision, and forced it to develop new neural pathways. Her disorders will have disappeared, her emotions manageable and more stable. It may be too soon to congratulate myself, but I did so well on my first attempt.

Of course, I won't know the results until she wakes up, and I speak with her. But unlike Dr. Halstead's patients, she didn't hemorrhage or seize on the table.

I'll take that as a good sign.

CHAPTER TWENTY-FIVE
OLIVIA

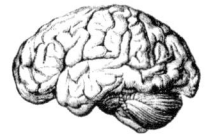

Consciousness.

I'm awake, but everything feels strange.

Unfamiliar.

My head aches like I've been hit with something, and as I bring my hand to my forehead, the skin is tender, and sore. My limbs are weak, heaviness blanketing my entire body. The quiet is suffocating as I search my mind for answers, a gnawing feeling in the pit of my stomach.

Who am I?

Where am I?

Do I have amnesia?

Panic rises in my chest, nausea churning in my belly. Was there an accident? Where are my memories?

My eyes slowly open, a soft light filling the room but it's still too bright, causing a piercing pain in the front of my skull. My gaze tracks the details of the room, but nothing rings a bell. I'm lying on a soft bed, surrounded by gray walls, dark wooden furniture in the corners of the large space.

Confusion leads to terror, and tears spring to my eyes. I have no idea what's going on, and nothing makes sense. Words and thoughts come easily, but they're the only things I have. Trying to recall a single memory from any part of my life is proving impossible.

There's nothing.

A dark void raising more questions than I already had upon opening my eyes.

Turning my head to the side, the source of light comes from a small lamp sitting atop a nightstand. As I look to the other side of the bed, a man sits in a chair, his eyes closed, sleeping. My body flinches.

Who is he?

Have I been kidnapped?

Has he hurt me?

Is he going to hurt me?

My chest tightens, fear and dread shooting through me so forcefully, I'd fall if I weren't already lying down.

Bracing my upper body on trembling hands, I push myself up, leaning against a cold, iron headboard. The man stirs in the chair as the bed squeaks, his eyes snapping open. He doesn't move a muscle as his dark gaze pins me to the spot, intense and assessing.

"You're awake." His deep voice is raspy from sleep, and it sends a shiver down my spine.

"Who are you?" I whisper, my throat dry and scratchy.

He leans forward, propping his elbows on his knees, his hands clasped together in front of him. "My name is Andrew Chambers. I'm not going to hurt you."

Tears form in my eyes, his face becoming blurry. "Why can't I remember my name?"

He gives me a sad smile. "Your name is Lilly. You were in a

car accident. You suffered a head injury which caused memory loss. You were recovering well in the hospital, and I brought you home. Unfortunately, you had a fainting spell. I took you back to the hospital, and they checked you out, but the doctor couldn't find anything. Only time will tell if your memories return."

His response has me spiraling into despair, but one word caught my attention above the others. "Home? Do w-we live here together?" I clear my throat to relieve the hoarseness, but it makes me cough, a throbbing pain piercing my head between my eyes.

He stands from his chair, pouring a glass of water from a pitcher on the nightstand. He holds the glass out for me to take, and I notice a wedding band on his ring finger. I hesitate for a moment before reaching for the glass, gasping as I see a matching band on my own finger. "Are we-" Words fail me as true panic settles in, paralyzing me.

He takes a seat in the chair. "Lilly, look at me."

This can't be real.

Wake up, Lilly.

My own name sounds foreign in my head, and the tears I'd been trying to hold back fall freely.

"Lilly." He tries again, and this time, I force my eyes to his. "Your name is Lilly Chambers."

The sob that leaves my chest is soul shattering, and I shake my head back and forth, denying the words before he speaks them.

He takes the glass of water from my hand, placing it on the nightstand. "We're married, Lilly. I'm your husband, and you're my wife."

"No!" I shout, my entire body shaking uncontrollably. I rip the blankets off my legs, moving to stand from the bed. My knees buckle, but he bolts from his chair, catching me before I hit the floor. Trying to push him away, he won't let go, and I slam my fists against his chest, sobbing until I finally collapse in his arms. He sits me on the edge of the bed, kneeling on the floor in front of me.

He grips my hands, holding them tightly as I cry. "It's going to be okay, little doll. I'm going to take care of you."

He doesn't speak for long minutes, allowing me to mourn a life I don't remember. As the last of the tears fade, he stands, moving around the room. He returns a moment later with the glass of water, holding it out to me like a peace offering. I take it, appreciating the cool liquid as it slides down my parched throat. Once I've finished it, he takes the glass, placing it next to the pitcher.

"W-will you t-tell me everything?" I stammer through the hiccups racking my chest.

"Of course." He reaches for my hand, and I don't pull away. "Rest, and we'll talk when you wake up."

I want to know everything now, but in the ten minutes I've been awake, the little bit of energy I had has been depleted. I'm asleep before the door latches when he leaves the room.

CHAPTER TWENTY-SIX
ATLAS

My neck is fucking killing me.

I stayed in her room after she fell asleep. While I wanted to make sure she was alright, I also needed to confirm she wouldn't have an episode or try to run.

She'll have a million questions for me today, so I already have the fake documents in hand confirming her new identity. It should help ease her anxiety, giving her something she can physically hold onto, a token of the life she doesn't remember.

Slowly twisting the knob, I open the door, careful not to wake her. It's a waste of effort. Emerald eyes stop me in my tracks as she stares at my face as soon as I enter the bedroom. She's laying on her side, the blanket pulled up to her chin. There's no sign of tears, thankfully.

I'm not sure I have the patience for that shit with this crick in my neck.

She turns over onto her back before easing herself in an upright position, leaning against the headboard. As I reach the edge of the bed, I hand her the documents. She reviews them carefully while I pour her a glass of water. As soon as this awkward conversation is over, I'll need to make her something to eat. Now that she's away from the asylum, I'll be able to put some weight on her.

Taking a seat in the chair that I slept in last night, I wait patiently as she shuffles through the paperwork. At least a dozen different emotions cross her face as she reads over her new birth certificate, the report from the car accident, our marriage certificate, and a social security card. Once she's finished, she lays it all on the nightstand, reaching for the water. She sips it for a few moments before setting it down.

"How did we meet?" She whispers, picking at a loose thread on the blanket.

Pretending the nostalgia is affecting me, I grin thoughtfully. "I'm a prosecutor in Grimdale County. I stopped in a little coffee shop on my way to the office one morning. I was distracted, thinking about the case I was working on, but a sweet, little voice broke through my chaotic thoughts. When I gave the barista my attention, I wasn't prepared for her to be the most beautiful girl I'd ever seen. She had beautiful, red hair that reminded me of autumn. And gorgeous, emerald eyes that I was immediately lost in."

Olivia leans towards me, completely captivated by this ridiculous story. I chose to go with something sweet and innocent. I know how women love those *Hallmark* movies.

There's a spark in her eyes as she hangs on every word I say, so I continue laying it on thick. "The girl was out of my league, but I took a chance, asking her on a date. Of course, she was shy and declined. But I made it my morning routine for weeks to stop by the coffee shop and see her."

Her eyes glisten with unshed tears as she listens to me spin a revolting tale of love at first sight.

"I woke up late one morning, and I didn't have time to stop by. Seeing her was the bright spot in my day, so you can only imagine how that one went." When a ghost of a smile tugs at her lips, I know I'm on the right track. "The next day, I stopped by, and when I asked her for a date again, she accepted. We went on a picnic, and to the town fair. It was a magical night, and we were inseparable after that. We were married a year later." I smile. "And we lived happily ever after until-" I drop my head in my hands, letting her feel the despair I'm projecting.

"Until?" She asks, her voice strained from lack of using it.

"Until the accident. Lilly, I don't think you're ready to hear this. I don't know if I'm ready to relive it." I give her a pleading look, knowing it will tug at her heart.

"Please? I need to know."

Exhaling heavily, I find her gaze. "You were driving home from work. It was storming heavily, and you hydroplaned. The car spun out of control, and you crashed into a tree. You hit your head on the steering wheel, hard." Moving from the chair to the edge of the bed, I'm surprised when she doesn't shrink back. "When I got the call, I thought I'd lost you. I was out of my mind by the time I reached the hospital. You were there for weeks. They released you once the swelling went down, and all your vitals and scans were normal. Once we were home, you were doing great, then something happened. You fainted, and as I told you yesterday, they couldn't find anything wrong. The doctor told us it would take time, but there's a chance your memories may not return."

She sniffles, wiping away her tears. "What about my family? Your family? I know nothing of my life."

"Lilly, we have plenty of time to go over all this. I think you should rest."

"No!" She shouts. My eyes widen, and she immediately looks remorseful. "I'm sorry. I can handle this. Please tell me."

Reaching for her hand, she allows me to intertwine our fingers. "I'm estranged from my family. I didn't have a happy childhood, and I chose to walk away once I was of age." There's sympathy in her eyes, and I continue. "You're an only child. Your mom passed away when you were little, and you lost your father two years ago."

"How?" She chokes out.

Fuck. She's full of questions. I'm glad I had all this planned out in my head.

"Your mother was hit head on by a drunk driver. Your father passed away from cancer."

She squeezes my fingers, and I shift further up the bed, taking her into my arms. "Shhh, little doll. They both loved you very much."

She pulls away, wiping the tears from her cheeks. She's so fucking beautiful when she cries, it makes my cock twitch.

Now is definitely not the time.

"You're all I have in this world," she states, and I kiss the top of her head.

That's what loving husbands do, right?

"And I'm all you'll ever need."

She gazes at me like I'm her only lifeline, which is the one sliver of truth in this entire situation. After a few moments, she lays her head on my chest. "I'm so lost."

"You're not lost, little doll. I found you the day I walked into that coffee shop five years ago, and I'm never letting you go. We'll get through this."

"Why do you call me little doll?"

Running my fingers through her hair, I give her a tiny truth. "Your pale skin reminds me of a porcelain doll. You're so beautiful."

She pulls away as if I've made her uncomfortable, and I let her go. "I think I'll rest now."

"Of course." I say as I rise from the bed. "I'll have dinner ready when you wake up."

"Thank you," she whispers as I leave the room.

CHAPTER TWENTY-SEVEN
OLIVIA

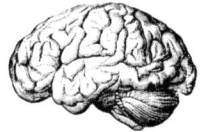

It's been a week since I woke up to my new life.

Andrew and I are coexisting well as we navigate through this mess. He told me he put in vacation time to be with me until he's confident I'm alright. We spend our days getting to know each other again. He tells me I'm still the same woman I've always been, my personality and my beauty still everything he wants. When he says those things, I can't help but feel close to him. But every time those feelings surface, the fact I can't remember my past overshadows any glimmer of happiness for my future.

He told me before the accident I worked at his law office. I'd taken courses to become a paralegal, and he insisted I work with him. I jokingly asked if we ever got tired of each other, but he didn't find humor in it. His eyes darkened dangerously, and he reiterated over and over how he'd be with me twenty-four hours a day if he could.

My instincts screamed that my husband is an intense and protective man, but his words also made me feel safe and loved. He hasn't touched me since the day he told me how we met, and about my family. I'm not sure why, but I did pull away from him before he left the room. While his touch soothed me, helping me through the shock of having my life told to me by a stranger, I was overwhelmed, and needed some space. He hasn't tried again.

It's obvious to me why I fell in love with Andrew, and why I married him. He's a beautiful man with a kind heart, and the patience of a saint. He cares for me like I'm a fragile little doll. The thought makes me smile, wondering if that's the true meaning for the endearment.

"Lilly." His voice startles me, and I spin around from the laundry I'm folding on the bed.

A shiver runs down my spine as I take him in. My breath catches as my eyes wander his bare chest, and down his torso, catching every dip and ridge of his muscular form. Gray sweatpants hang low on his hips, deep muscles disappearing beneath the material.

He's truly male perfection.

"Lilly." His voice deepens, and our gazes clash as he begins moving closer. He doesn't stop until he's directly in front of me, our bodies a mere inch apart.

My body comes alive, desperately craving his touch, and I bite my bottom lip to stifle a whimper. His pupils dilate, and I gasp as he leans in, our lips almost touching. "I think you grabbed some of my laundry, little doll."

My mouth is suddenly dry, and I swallow slowly. "I'm s-sorry."

He smirks. "No need, sweetheart. I just need a shirt."

I turn quickly to dig through the pile of clothes. My body tenses as his chest presses against my back, his arm coming around my waist, plucking a black t-shirt from the mound. He lingers a few moments, burying his nose in my hair, inhaling deeply. He grips my hip, his fingers digging into my skin, and I press my lips together to suppress a moan.

"You smell fucking divine." He groans, and a desperate noise escapes my throat, my cheeks flushing with embarrassment. His lips ghost down my neck, and my body begins to tremble. "So responsive to my touch."

This man has me under his spell, and before I question what I'm doing, I spin around to face him. The intensity in his eyes has desire pooling in my lower belly, and when his lips brush the shell of my ear, my core clenches. "Andrew."

He kisses my cheek, before pulling away. "I'll have breakfast ready in a bit."

I nod slowly, watching him as he slips the shirt over his head before leaving the room. As soon as he's out of sight, all the oxygen rushes back into the room, and I feel like I can breathe again.

"Do you think we could go somewhere today?" I ask, after rinsing my plate.

He takes it from my hand, drying it with the dish towel. "Not yet. You're still healing."

"Oh."

He places the plate in the cabinet, facing me once he's closed the door. "Your injury is quite complex, little doll. You need peace and quiet to heal properly. I don't want you exposed to the outside world full of stress and anxiety until we know you've recovered properly."

"I just thought it'd be nice to get out of the house," I whisper, wiping down the counter.

He sighs. "It will be. Once you're better."

"I understand."

He steps behind me, wrapping his arms around my middle. He props his chin on my shoulder, nuzzling his nose against the side of my neck. His touch sends a shiver down my spine, and I turn in his arms, our lips dangerously close.

"You're very protective." I whisper.

"Fuck yes," he growls, and the sound causes goosebumps to erupt across my skin.

He leans in, his lips ghosting over mine, and I gasp, the faint touch setting my body on fire. Lifting up onto my toes, I press my mouth to his, and he groans, his fingers digging into my waist, pulling me closer. His tongue pushes past my lips, and I moan, pressing myself against him, wanting more.

Needing more.

His kiss is just as intense as his dark eyes, and he owns me in a way that has me panting against his mouth. Our tongues tangle in a desperate dance, and my hips grind against him, his hard cock so close to where I want him.

He pulls away abruptly, and I suck in a lungful of air, slowly opening my eyes. He's watching me, his gaze darting between my eyes and lips. "I'm going to shower."

I blink. "Oh. Okay."

He leaves the kitchen coolly, and I stare at his back as he walks away wondering what the hell just happened.

CHAPTER TWENTY-EIGHT
ATLAS

O livia is driving me fucking crazy.

I've told her countless times she can't leave the house until she's fully recovered. While that may be true to an extent, my primary reason for her captivity is so no one realizes she isn't actually dead. I live far enough from the asylum that it's highly improbable someone will recognize her, but I'm still cautious, and paranoid as fuck.

It's been almost a month since she awoke from the lobotomy, and she asks every few days if we can go somewhere. I'm almost sympathetic to her cause, especially when she asks to simply ride down the back roads in the car.

Not happening.

She'll stay in this cage until I work out the details of our relocation. It'll sadden me to leave the asylum, but there's others across the country that would be lucky to have my expertise. It will also give us the distance to live a normal life where we can leave home together without someone recognizing her.

I'll need to install a tracker under her skin before that happens.

She's going stir crazy, and while I understand her frustration, I'm not badgering her every few days, whining about my hard cock not being taken care of.

I've succeeded in being a loving husband, a good provider, and a shoulder to cry on when she has one of her frequent crying episodes. What else do I have to do in order for her to give herself over to me completely?

I had her hot and bothered in the kitchen a few days ago, but I'm a little too old for a dry humping session.

I want her to come to me.

Beg me for it.

My patience is wearing thin, and I honestly don't know how men handle this shit. Always initiating sex. It's exhausting. With everything I've done for her, you'd think she'd bow at my feet, her body at my disposal anytime I want.

Fucking women.

The lobotomy was supposed to cure the unappealing bits of her personality, instead it's created new ones. Sometimes I find myself missing the violent little thing who stood toe to toe with anyone, including me.

I guess the past has a way of coming back to haunt us.

I pulled into the driveway about ten minutes ago, and I'm surprised she hasn't come outside yet. She usually meets me at the door, says she can hear me when I pull up. Rubbing at my temples, I tell myself this woman was meant for me, no matter how obnoxious she is at times.

She's beautiful, fiery, and while she may fray my last nerve some days, others I don't want to live without her.

Maybe I'm just irritable because my cock is being neglected.

A month without her tight cunt wrapped around me is too long.

Opening the car door, I grab my briefcase, one that she thinks belongs to a successful lawyer. I cross the yard, climbing the steps onto the porch. As I open the door, an old record plays, and a smile tugs at my lips knowing she's been into my collection.

Turning the corner into the kitchen, I stop dead in my tracks. She's wearing the tiniest pair of shorts I've ever seen, accompanied by a tight-fitted tank top. Her hair is pulled up into a messy bun, her bare feet sporting hot pink toenail polish she asked me to pick up a few days ago on my way home. She's swaying back and forth with the music, stirring something in a pot that smells incredible. I've been teaching her how to cook.

The smile quickly disappears as reality sinks in.

If I stay in this room any longer, I'll say or do something I may regret.

She chooses this particular moment to spin around, giving me a bright, genuine smile. "Hey you."

I nod. "Lilly."

She places the cooking utensil on the stove top, taking a few steps in my direction. "I hope you're hungry."

She's so hopeful. So clueless about the kind of man I truly am. I told myself I could live this life, be a loving and dutiful husband. But in this moment, all I want to do is throw her onto the floor and fuck her brains out.

What's left of it.

Her smile falls. "Are you okay?"

I'm torn between the man I'm pretending to be, and the man I am.

The man she despises.

"I've had a long day. I'm going to my bedroom. Good-night, Lilly."

She rushes forward, her hand gripping my forearm. The connection sends a lightning bolt straight to my cock, and I need to get as far away from her as possible before I *take* what I want.

"Do you want to talk-"

"No." My tone is harsh, and she retreats a few steps.

She looks heartbroken, and a part me takes joy in her pain.

I always have.

Her eyes become glassy, and I begin to walk away before I have to witness one of her fucking crying fits again.

CHAPTER TWENTY-NINE
OLIVIA

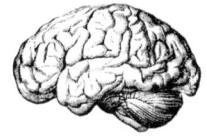

After tossing and turning for hours, I still can't go to sleep.

Something deep inside me aches for Andrew. He's upset, and it bothers me that as his wife, I don't know what to do. He went to bed without eating, and all I did was pick at my food until I finally got up, throwing it into the trash. A deep loneliness settled in my chest as I took a shower and slipped into bed.

He was harsh before leaving the kitchen, but he's probably stressed, and my situation isn't making things any easier.

I should go to him, shouldn't I?

My memories of our previous relationship may be nonexistent, but I have feelings for him now, and I want to soothe whatever has him so stressed.

Untangling myself from the blanket, I pad across the floor, slipping from the bedroom. The hall is dark, but there is a faint stream of light peeking from underneath his door. My nerves have me on the verge of running back to my room, but I stand firm as I raise my knuckles to the wood, knocking softly.

"Come in," he calls.

Opening the door, I enter his room, and all the air rushes from my lungs. He's sitting up in bed, relaxed against the headboard, the blanket pulled up to his waist. He's shirtless, and my mouth waters as I take in his toned chest and abdomen, ridges defining his muscular upper body. His hair is damp from a shower, his tanned skin flushed, most likely from scalding his knotted muscles.

"Did you need something, Lilly?" He interrupts my thoughts.

My body trembles with awareness, my core aching for friction and pressure. I clear my throat. "Which room was *our* room?"

He blinks as if my question caught him off guard. "The one you're sleeping in. Why?"

His eyes darken as I approach his side of the bed. Gripping the edge of the blanket, I pull it back, grateful he's wearing a pair of briefs. It'd be extremely awkward if he'd been naked.

He doesn't speak as I take his hand, tugging him up. He obliges, following me out of the room, as I lead him to *our* bedroom.

Letting go of his hand, I climb into bed, my body vibrating with nerves. Pulling back the blanket, I watch him as he gazes at me from the doorway. "I'd like for you to stay in here with me."

He tilts his head. "Why, little doll?"

My stomach sinks. "You don't have to. I just thought maybe-"

He stalks to the side of the bed, gripping my chin with his fingers. "Tell me why, Lilly."

"Something is bothering you, and I'm your wife. You should be in here with me."

I gasp as he places his palm on my chest, pushing me down onto the mattress. He crawls over me, and I bite back a moan as his weight pins me for a brief moment before he shifts onto his side. Desire for my husband hits me like a ton of bricks, and suddenly I can't think of anything other than his body pressed against mine.

He grips my waist with one hand, rolling me onto my side to face him. My breath quickens as our lips hover a few inches apart.

"Bad day, little doll," he whispers.

"Do you want to talk about it? Is there anything I can do?" He watches my mouth as I speak, and as I try to be a good wife, and console my husband, every thought running through my mind begins and ends with his hands on me.

He shifts closer, and my thighs clench as the scent of his spicy body wash fills my lungs. "Are *you* okay? You seem tense." His lips brush my jaw, the light touch torturous.

"I'm fine," I whisper.

"Hmmm." He hums, sending a shiver down my spine. "Do you want to kiss me, Lilly?" I nod my head, and he smirks, knowing exactly what he's doing to me. "I'm all yours."

I don't give my brain time to come up with some logical reason why I shouldn't rush this.

Andrew is mine, and I want him.

Leaning forward, I press my lips to his. His grip tightens on my hip, as his other hand snakes around my neck, fisting the hair at the base of my skull. His tongue licks the seam of my lips, and as I open for him, his chest rumbles with a sound so masculine, I melt against him. He pushes me onto my back, and I moan as he settles his weight between my thighs, caging me in with his forearms on either side of my head. "Fuck, I've missed this."

His words make my chest ache. How the hell I ever forgot this feeling is beyond me. Sadness threatens to consume me with all the things I don't remember.

He pulls away, searching my face. "Do you want me?"

A pang of guilt twists in my gut, hating that I made him doubt how I feel. "Yes."

He cups my cheek with his palm, and I nuzzle into his touch. "I need you so fucking badly, Lilly. But if you're not ready-"

"I'm ready," I blurt out, and he cocks an eyebrow. "I got lost in my head for a minute."

"What were you thinking about?"

My cheeks heat, but I tell him the truth. "I don't know how I could ever forget this."

He grins. "Oh really?"

I slap his chest. "Don't get cocky."

His eyes darken, the intensity almost too much to bear. "I'm going to keep you in this bed, fucking you for days until you're begging me to stop. I'm going to use you, break you, and when you regain consciousness, I'll do it all over again."

My mouth is suddenly dry at his delicious threat. My mind can't conjure a single response, so I do the only thing I can. Wrapping my arms around his neck, I pull him down as I crash our lips together.

He growls, the vibration going straight to my pussy. My hips rise, seeking the friction I so desperately need, but he chuckles against my mouth. "So impatient."

His hand leaves my hip, slipping lower, sliding inside the waistband of my sleep shorts. I gasp as he trails a single finger across my panties, tracing my seam through the drenched fabric. He pushes them to the side, sinking a finger inside me. "You're fucking soaked."

A whimper escapes me as he withdraws, only to add another one. My hips buck into his hand, begging for release. "Please."

"That's it, little doll. Fuck yourself on my fingers," he mutters against my lips before trailing his tongue across my jaw, sucking and nipping a path down my neck. "Be a good girl. Come on my hand, and I'll give you my cock."

He's so fucking arrogant, but it works for me. My lower belly coils tightly, my legs shaking uncontrollably. Indecent noises leave my lips, but I can't bring myself to be embarrassed. I'm teetering on the brink of oblivion, but I need something more. "Harder. Please."

"So fucking pretty when you beg." He groans, pressing his thumb against my clit, the pressure sending me over the edge.

Crying out his name, my body arches off the bed, my hips grinding against his skilled fingers. He whispers praises in my ear, his warm breath sending a wave of awareness across my skin. He circles my clit slowly, dragging every ounce of pleasure from my limp body.

As I lie motionless, my limbs tingling, my skin flushed, he slides his fingers from my pussy, bringing them to his mouth. My lips part as I watch him suck them clean, his tongue catching what's sliding down his palm, his eyes closed as if he's experiencing pleasure the way I just did.

My thighs clench around his waist, and his eyes fly open, full of danger and darkness. "I can't wait to stuff your tight pussy with my tongue. But that will have to wait. I need you wrapped around my cock."

He rises from the bed, gripping the waistband of my shorts, jerking them down my legs along with my panties. He discards them onto the floor before doing the same with his briefs. My lips part as I unabashedly stare at his cock, both fascinated, and terrified. He's long and thick, a large vein traveling the entire length of his shaft. Licking my lips, I reach for it, but he bats my hand away.

He moves onto the bed, crawling up my body, trailing his thumb across my bottom lip. "There'll be time for that later, little doll. I look forward to fucking that beautiful face of yours." He kisses me fast and hard before rising to his knees, spreading my thighs wider. He stares between my legs, his pupils dilating. "So swollen and pink. You're dripping for me, aren't you?"

"Yes." I moan, wiggling my hips, begging to be filled.

His thumbs spread me open as he pushes the head of his cock inside me. My pussy stretches, a burning sensation traveling through my core. The pain only intensifies the pleasure, and my eyes roll back in my head. He withdraws, sliding back in further this time. My back arches, and I feel like I may lose consciousness. He withdraws once more, but I don't have time to feel hollow or empty. He slams into me, ripping a scream from my throat. He pauses, that cocky smirk on his lips once again. "Too much?"

"Yes!" I pant, already addicted to the pain. "Don't stop."

The rumble in his chest combined with the feral look in his eyes has me wrapping my legs around his waist, crossing my ankles behind his back. He falls forward, catching his weight on his forearms. He brings his hand to the top of my head, fisting my hair. His other hand flies to my throat, his long fingers pressing into the sensitive skin of my neck. "Don't fucking let go."

Oh. God.

He slides out slowly, his eyes on my face, watching me for a moment before driving into me again.

It's the last break I get.

"Remember how much I care for you, Lilly." He grins. "It's about to feel like I don't."

A strangled cry is torn from my throat as he fucks me like my only purpose in this world is to take his cock. His grip on my hair is painful. His hold on my throat is unforgiving. The brutal pace of his hips is my undoing. I come so fucking hard, tears spring to my eyes. My nails dig into his back, the pain making him groan, and his hips snap back and forth harder, faster.

"You're gripping me so tight," he grounds out, his jaw clenched.

"More." I beg before my body has a chance to recover.

My overstimulated body is weak and useless, but I'd happily lie here while he fucks me into a coma. I can't get enough of him.

He pulls out abruptly, flipping me onto my stomach. He grips my hips roughly, pulling me onto my hands and knees. "Hold onto the headboard."

I do as I'm told, my fingers clenching around the iron rods so tightly, my knuckles turn white. He drives his cock inside me so hard, my body rocks forward, my grip on the headboard the only thing stopping my head from crashing into it.

"Oh fuck!" I scream, tears steadily streaming down my face.

He jerks my face to the side. "So pretty when you cry for me, little doll."

"You're so deep. It's too much." I sob, meeting his thrusts as he uses my body.

He gathers my hair in one hand, jerking my head back as he leans down, his lips against my ear. "Such a good little whore for your husband." He slams into me over and over, his grunts of pleasure making me clench around him so tightly, it's painful. "You like being my fuck toy don't you, little doll? You'll be raw and useless by the time I'm finished with you."

His filthy mouth has me spiraling once again, but this time he comes with me. He roars like an animal as he fills my abused pussy with his cum, slowly thrusting, dragging out every ounce of pleasure between us. I collapse onto the mattress, and he follows, shifting onto his side beside me. He pulls me into his arms, cradling my head in the crook of his neck. "You're perfect."

It's the last thing I hear before sleep takes me.

CHAPTER THIRTY
ATLAS

I t's been too long since I've tasted her sweet pussy.

She's asleep, lying on her back, and I slowly pull open her thighs, my shoulders pinning them wide. My fingers spread open her abused pussy, my tongue fucking her swollen hole.

Fuck.

Her flavor is intoxicating, a combination of both of us. It goes straight to my head, and I'm cum-drunk, stabbing my tongue inside her, stretching the appendage to consume every drop I can find.

My fingers dig into her soft flesh as I circle her clit, pulling a sweet moan from her lips. She tenses for a moment but relaxes as I circle her opening with one finger, barely dipping it inside. She rocks her hips, begging for more, but I don't give in, driving her as crazy as she does me.

It's imperative she feels a fraction of the madness I've

experienced these last few weeks, waiting for her to find her way back to me. I'm making an effort to be the man she needs, but my patience was slipping when I came home last night.

"Andrew, don't tease me," she begs, and I long to hear her cry out *my* name.

I miss my true identity on her lips, her sweet cries for me. *Atlas*.

Pushing two fingers deep inside her, I curl them upwards, hitting the spot that always makes her come. She cries out, fueling my desire, the threads of my control fraying. Nipping her clit, I finger fuck her pussy hard and fast until she's clenching around me, screaming. I rip my fingers free from her vise-like grip, her tight hole expanding before she squirts all over my face, dripping onto the sheets beneath us.

My tongue darts out, catching the liquid, groaning as my cock twitches in response. Crawling up her body, her eyes open, dazed and unfocussed. "Good morning, little doll."

"Good morning," she whispers, her cheeks flushing as I lean down, taking her mouth in a slow kiss.

"My cock wants inside here," I murmur against her lips, and she gasps. "Do you want me to fuck your face?" I kiss her again, my tongue lazily stroking her mouth. "Do you want to choke on my cock, sweet girl?"

Her body begins to tremble, and she nods. "Show me how."

"So fucking obedient." I grin. "Stay as you are. I'll talk you through it."

She nods again, and I place a knee beside each of her shoulders. Palming my cock, I pump it twice, guiding it to her lips. "Open."

She obeys beautifully, sticking out her tongue. Sliding inside her warm mouth is something I can't put into words.

I imagine it's heaven and hell, if there were such a thing.

Her lips stretch around me, the sight causing my hips to

punch forward, and she chokes. I pull back, allowing her to breathe for a moment. Gripping the top of the headboard, I angle my hips, pushing further into her mouth. She relaxes, taking me easier, as I fuck her throat deeper. She moans, hollowing her cheeks, creating a delicious suction around me.

"That's it, little doll. Swallow my cock like a good girl," I grit out, clenching my jaw to keep from embarrassing myself already. I don't know where she learned to suck dick, but she hardly feels inexperienced. Her stepbrother was the only sexual encounters she had before me. We were together a handful of times at the asylum. But right now, she feels like a fucking porn star trying to suck my soul through my cock.

She's exactly what I want.

Thrusting my hips, I fuck her face just as hard and fast as I fuck her cunt. The tiny noises she's making have me gripping the headboard so tightly, I feel like I could snap the iron rod in half. Delicate fingers caress my balls, and the breath rushes out of my lungs as she gives them a firm tug. "Fuck!"

She does it again, a tingling sensation gathering at the base of my spine. She looks up at me from beneath her lashes, and the trail of tears cascading down her face mixed with the drool leaking from the corners of her mouth are my undoing. My balls tighten, my cock slightly swelling before I drive down her throat for the final time, shooting my cum down her throat. She swallows every drop, and as I slip from between her lips, she breathes deeply.

Making my way down the mattress, my eyes catch on her needy cunt, swollen and begging to be filled. My cock hardens again as I grip her hips, flipping her onto her belly. I don't give her time to process what's happening as I slam inside her, my eyes rolling back in my head. I'm still sensitive, and the feeling of her wrapped around me has my legs shaking involuntarily.

My gaze lands on her perfect ass, bouncing as I fuck her hard, her screams and pleas fueling the monster inside me.

Saliva drips from my tongue, landing on her asshole, and I use my finger to push it inside. She tenses, but I don't stop. A deep moan leaves her lips as I add another finger. "I'm about to fuck your tight ass, little doll."

She whimpers as I pull out of her dripping pussy, notching the head of my cock at her back hole. I take it easy on her, pushing inside slowly, giving her time to adjust. She watches me over her shoulder, tears leaking from her eyes, and my hips shoot forward, filling her completely. She screams, and I give her two seconds of reprieve before I begin a punishing rhythm. She's a crying, blubbering mess, but her hips match mine, thrust for thrust.

"That's my girl. You like my cock in your ass? You want to be my good, little slut, don't you?"

She whimpers, and I slip two fingers inside her sloppy cunt, her arousal making it easy to slip in a third. I've filled all her holes in a matter of minutes, and she's still begging for more. Olivia was meant to be my little whore from the moment I first saw her.

Perfectly packaged to satisfy my cock.

My thumb presses against her clit, my fingers slipping in and out of her as I drive my cock into her ass. It's the perfect storm for an orgasm so powerful, she'll never forget who she belongs to. She screams my name as her body locks up, her ass clenching around me so tightly, I have no choice but to succumb to my own release. I pump her so full of cum, it leaks out around me as I slowly thrust in and out of her tight hole.

She collapses onto the mattress, and I do the same beside her, pulling her into my arms. While I'm not into feelings, and all the emotional shit, I do enjoy holding her.

She turns over, trailing her fingers across my cheek, down the center of my throat. She smiles shyly. "You know what the perfect ending to this shameful morning activity would be?"

"I believe we just experienced the perfect ending." I grin as she smacks me on the chest.

"A drive on the back roads with the windows down, enjoying the fresh air."

The euphoric afterglow ends abruptly.

Not this shit again.

After the fucking I just gave her, you'd think she'd be compliant, not fucking annoying.

Rolling out of bed, I slide on my briefs before leaving the room, seething at her audacity.

She should be grateful.

Content.

Instead, she always wants more. She's never satisfied.

"Andrew!" She shouts, hurried footsteps sounding on the hardwood floor behind me.

Spinning around, I grip her biceps as she attempts to stop before crashing into me. "Am I not enough? Do I not treat you well? Give you everything you need? Stay by your side?" My anger is rising to a dangerous boiling point; one Olivia has never witnessed in this new life or the last.

"What?" She rears back as if I've slapped her.

"You're always trying to leave!" I shout before storming through the house once again.

I need some fucking space before I do something I can't take back.

CHAPTER THIRTY-ONE
OLIVIA

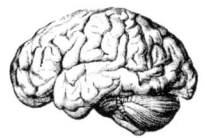

I'm hot on his heels, following him through the house, gripping his forearm as he enters the foyer. "I'm tired of being trapped in this house."

He jerks out of my hold. "You don't need to leave. Didn't you learn your lesson after the accident?"

"You think I wanted to get hurt? Lose my memory? Get to know my husband again? I had to relearn my fucking life!" It's getting hard to breathe as I feel the walls closing in on me. "Fuck this! I'm leaving." I'm in a t-shirt and sleep shorts with his cum leaking down my thighs, but I don't give a fuck. I have to get away from him. Heading for the front door, he grabs my wrist painfully, and I whirl around, slapping him across the face. "Don't fucking touch me!"

Running towards the door, I yelp as he fists my hair, snatching my head back. "You're not going anywhere. You belong to me." He sneers as he pins me against the wall.

"Fuck you!" I scream at the top of my lungs. I didn't know I had that in me, but damn it felt good.

His cold eyes meet mine for a split second before he back-hands me across the face so hard my body falls sideways, my forehead hitting the corner of the entryway table. My vision blurs, piercing, blinding pain shooting through my head.

My hands dart out to break the fall, but in my disoriented state, I land face first on the hardwood floor, pain exploding through my head once again. I cry out, but the sound is distant, muffled by a high pitch ringing in my ears.

The world around me darkens, the throbbing in my head intensifying. I'm screaming, but there's no sound. The ringing stops, an eerie quiet filling the air, cocooning me in silence. Little specs of light float across my vision.

Am I dead?

Lying motionless, my eyes dart between the bright spots, and my breathing stops as each illuminated point shifts into a scene, one at a time.

Memories.

Each light represents a memory from my life before, and I'm plunged into my past, both startled and horrified.

So. Much. Blood.

I'm paralyzed as I watch each segment unfold, like watching an old movie on a projector.

I'm stabbing a woman with a fire poker.

Then a man.

The shower.

Choking a younger guy with his…

Oh. My. God.

They were my family.

Memories of my stepbrother assaulting me.

A hospital.

An older man trying to help me.

Another hospital.

No. A prison.

Atlas.

Us together.

My vision darkens again, the specs of light dimming, only to return larger and more blinding than before. The deep throbbing launches behind my eyes, snaking through the center of my skull. It's deep and steady, growing fiercer by the second. A murderous scream echoes in my mind as another series of memories assault me.

Shock therapy.

Needles.

A plan for my release.

Halstead stabbed me.

And Atlas. He watched.

He…

Lobotomy.

Large hands grip my shoulders, shaking me while screaming my name, though his desperate pleas sound far away. My eyes land on *his* face.

My doctor.

My tormentor.

My husband.

"Lilly! Can you hear me?" His panic almost seems genuine if I didn't remember who he is.

What he's done.

Planting my hands firmly on the floor, I fight the wave of dizziness as I push myself up. He grips my arms, helping me to stand, leading me to the couch. I don't speak a word as he kneels before me, inspecting the wound on my forehead. "I'm so sorry, little doll."

Bile rises in my throat. The endearment that made me feel safe and cared for is just another claim of his ownership. He's the one in control, and I'm just an insignificant piece in his fucked game.

None of it was real.

We aren't really married. The ring weighing heavily on

my finger is just another manipulation. Another carefully thought out move in his game of deceit and betrayal.

"Kill him." I startle at the familiar voice in my head. I'm stunned, taking a few moments to piece things together. It all falls into place, and I grin. *"Hello old friend."* I think to myself, comfort and a sense of home warming my entire body.

Atlas's voice fades away once again as my body heats, a sheen of sweat forming across my forehead. The throbbing in my skull takes a backseat to the onslaught of memories I'm sorting through. They all come back at once, and my system overloads as twenty years of despair playback in a matter of minutes. While the specs of light from earlier began with the murder of my family, the quiet whisper in my head has unleashed everything.

I remember.

My vision tunnels as the full force of my rage crawls out from the recesses of my mind. Death slithers through my chest, wrapping itself around my soul. It's beautiful, razor-sharp thorns pierce my heart, the vines they're attached to encasing the organ like an impenetrable shield protecting me from the world.

It's fucking liberating.

My eyes scan the room, catching sight of a fire poker by the fireplace.

Full circle.

"Lilly," he says my name with so much emotion; it makes me want to slit his throat.

Lifting my hand slowly, I run my fingers through his hair, fisting it as I reach the back of his head. I lean forward, our lips almost touching. "Atlas."

His entire body jerks back, his expression almost comical. For the first time since I've met him, he's speechless. Rising to his full height, he steps back, allowing me room to stand. My head is pounding, but I block it out and focus.

I'm not anxious.

I'm not terrified.

I'm not alone.

Embracing the furious bitch inside my mind, I let her soothe me like a mother coddling her newborn. A soft buzzing sensation travels the length of my body, a gentle caress guiding me into the darkness as it swallows me whole.

This is where I belong.

"Olivia." His voice interrupts my long-awaited transformation, and I brush past him, heading towards the fireplace.

The fire poker is at my back, and as I turn his way, our gazes collide like thunder and lightning. Tension fills the room, trapping us in a prison of lies and chaos. The air charges between us, and I stifle a laugh at the panic on his face.

While I'd rather kill him where he stands, I want answers. "Explain."

He takes a step towards me but thinks better of it, his shoulders deflating. "Olivia, please remain calm. Listen to what I have to say," he pleads, raising his palms in surrender.

"Now, Atlas."

He sighs, running his hands down his face. "Olivia Sterling is dead." He gauges my reaction, and when I give him nothing, he continues. "Halstead told me to get rid of you instead of saving you. He claimed your death was a suicide and filed for your death certificate."

I think back to that day in his office. The hopelessness I felt, the absolute finality of his words. I snapped, wanting nothing more than to tear his heart out for condemning me to a life of darkness and torture. As I relive every moment in his office, I'm reminded Atlas didn't try to help me.

He didn't intervene. He simply stood on the sidelines, enjoying the show.

He knew Halstead would never release me.

For the first time ever, I witness his perfectly crafted façade crumble beneath my gaze. He's normally so confident, so fucking arrogant. Seeing him like this is both surprising and quite amusing. "You knew I wouldn't walk out of his office free, didn't you?"

He sighs, running his fingers through his hair. "I couldn't tell you my plan, little doll. It would've ruined everything."

"Don't fucking call me that!" I shout. "You were willing to risk me dying for shits and giggles."

He takes a step forward. "No! I knew you would have an episode, and I knew he would hurt you. But I saved you, Olivia. It all went according to my plan. I got you out of that hell. We can be together now. Just you and me."

With a humorless laugh, I shake my head. "After everything you've done to me, do you think I'd willingly be with you? Is that why you gave me a fucking lobotomy? You knew it too, Atlas. That's why you scrambled my brain, so I'd forget all you've done."

He grits his teeth. "You need me. You can't survive without me. I'm the only one who can handle your episodes."

"Oh, yes. You handle me alright. You sedated me, electrocuted me, and rammed a fucking ice pick into my brain." I roll my eyes. "You're such a fuck up. You had me where you wanted me. Your little plan came together. And what did you do? You fucking hit me and look what happened." I chuckle. "It looks like the universe hates both of us."

He strides over, halting a foot in front of me. "I helped you. You can live a normal life. I'll take care of you, Olivia. I did what I had to do. For you."

This motherfucker is delusional.

He did everything because he took pleasure in torturing me, physically and psychologically.

He's a fucking monster.

He enjoys hurting people.

"You still work at the asylum, don't you?" He simply nods. "You only changed your name with me?" He nods again.

He closes the distance between us, tucking a few stray hairs behind my ear. I take a step back where the fire poker leans against the brick, carefully gripping it in my hand. Bringing it flush against my back, Atlas is too focused on petting my hair to notice.

"My beautiful, little doll. You've always belonged to me." His fingers move to my throat, wrapping around it firmly. "I'll fake your death." He leans in, burying his face in my hair. "I'll perform whatever procedure I see fit in order to keep you with me." He nips my earlobe, and I remember when his touch used to send a shiver down my spine.

Now, I want to vomit.

"I'll make you my prisoner." He trails his nose across my jaw, until his lips are a whisper against mine. "I'll do whatever the fuck I want to you. And do you know why?"

Shaking my head, I play the part of the broken, little doll he's used to.

"Because the day you were brought into the asylum, you became mine." He smirks.

Trailing my free hand up his chest, my palm comes to rest on his cheek. "Atlas."

He leans into my touch, and for a fleeting moment, a pang of guilt hits me in the chest.

He's the broken one.

Not me.

I'm a trauma survivor with mental illnesses, but even with those things working against me, I finally understand who I am. "I was falling in love with you. I was willing to give you everything if you would've treated me like a person, and not an experiment."

He grips my wrist, pulling it away from his face, kissing my palm. "If I were capable of love, Olivia, you would have it all."

"What is it you feel for me then?" I push.

"Obsession. You occupy every waking thought. I need to

know where you are at all times. No one will ever hurt you again."

I blink. "You're the only one who hurts me, Atlas."

It's his turn to blink, as if confused by my words. "But I enjoy your pain, little doll."

Pushing up on my tiptoes, I crash my lips to his. He pushes his tongue into my mouth, groaning as I deepen the kiss, pressing myself against his chest.

His kiss used to set my body on fire. In the asylum, I craved his attention, his touch. After I lost my memory, I let myself fall for him again, and the things he made me feel were borderline insanity.

I needed him.

Now, I hate his fucking guts.

I crave his blood.

"Kill him." Embracing the freedom in her words, it feels as though all my broken pieces are stitched back together, and for the first time in my life, I'm whole.

A phoenix rising from the ashes, the warmth of the smoldering embers building inside me. The pressure becomes heavy, igniting the flames of revenge and retribution. I'm death incarnate, and there's only one thing left to do.

Let go.

"I'll enjoy your pain as well, Dr. Stone." Taking a step back, I swing the fire poker around my front, plunging it into his abdomen, a squelching sound filling the air between us. He staggers back, gripping the iron rod with both hands, and I watch as true pain flickers across his face. I wrap my hand around the poker, ripping it from his gut, chunks of his insides dangling from the hook.

Is that a piece of his liver?

Maybe a bit of his kidney?

He falls to his knees, his hands flying to cover the wound as blood oozes out in a steady stream. Standing above him, I grip a handful of his perfectly styled hair, slamming my knee into his face. He howls, and I rear back, the full force of my fist connecting with his nose. The crunching of his bones is nothing short of satisfying. Squatting down in front of him, I lift his chin to meet my eyes. "Do you approve of the person I've become, *husband*?"

He's in excruciating agony, but the crazy bastard grins, his hand lifting to my face. "You're perfect, little doll." He coughs, blood spraying from his mouth, leaking down his chin, a crimson trail slowly running down his throat.

A foul smell invades my nostrils, and I realize I've punctured his intestines. "Your body is poisoning itself. Should I let you suffer the way you made me suffer? Or should I put you out of your misery?"

He hacks violently, the wheezing and gurgling forcing more blood from his mouth. He collapses onto his stomach, his life force pooling on the floor beneath him. Rising to my feet, I stand over him, the poker still in my hand.

He's so fucking pathetic.

Turning his head to the side, he stops hacking long enough to stutter out a few words. "I'm s-so proud of y-you." He attempts to clear his throat but ends up choking on more blood. "If I'm breathing, y-you'll never be f-free of m-me."

Even as he lies dying on the floor at my feet, he thinks he's still in control.

I'm in motherfucking control.

He's nothing. The big, bad tormentor is just another weak, little bitch, too prideful to admit he's lost at his own game.

Lifting the fire poker in front of me, I slam it down into the back of his neck, blood spraying my legs and waist from the force of the blow. I grit my teeth as the iron chafes against my palms, vibration from the impact rattling the small bones in my hands. Twisting it side to side, I don't stop until the wound is gaping before pulling it from his neck, tossing it to the floor beside him.

Sinking to my knees, I plop down on my ass next to him as he struggles for one last breath.

How the fuck is he still alive?

Isn't there something in the neck that kills you instantly if it's severed?

Stubborn bastard.

While my humanity far surpasses his, I can't seem to find it in me to console him or give him any inspirational words of hope for the afterlife. There's no bright light waiting for him at the end of a tunnel. No angels to open a pearly gate, allowing him to live in a pretty garden for all eternity.

Atlas Stone is a fucking monster with a one-way ticket to hell.

The devil himself will light the son-of-a-bitch on fire.

"Olivia," he breathes my name, his hand reaching for mine. I pull it away before he can touch me, and he grins one last time before expelling his final breath.

I hold my breath, watching him for a few moments, making sure the fucker is really dead. His body is still as a statue, but I press my finger into his cheek just to make sure.

Nothing.

Rolling him onto his back, his chest doesn't rise or fall, his extremities lying limply at unnatural angles. Pressing two fingers to the pulse point in his neck, I feel nothing.

He's dead.

It's finally over.

The uncertainty. The lies. The torture.

It all ended with his last breath, and I can't help but grin.

I'm fucking free.

I don't know what the next step will be, but I have a new identity, and with a little investigating, I'm sure I can get my hands on some of Atlas's money. The thought crosses my mind to take his phone, and send his black market contact a message. The only thing stopping me from offering up his organs for a nice payday is the fact no one deserves to have a single piece of him in their body.

Everything about Atlas Stone is infectious and rotten.

Pushing myself up from the floor, I wince at my stinging palms and aching head. The voice is quiet now, satiated by the death of its enemy.

I'm in desperate need of a shower, covered in blood and his cum. I'm headed that way until my stomach growls, steering my body towards the kitchen.

I'll deal with him later.

I'm in the mood for a sandwich.

CHAPTER THIRTY-TWO
OLIVIA

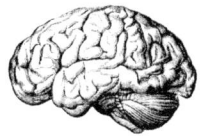

After eating a cold cut sandwich, I fell asleep in the chair while I contemplated what to do with Atlas's body.

I've killed people before, but it was during an IED episode, so I don't remember much. I never realized just how physically and emotionally draining it could be. Not only that, but I've never had to dispose of a corpse.

I'm still covered in blood, but I didn't see the point in showering until I've buried him. There are many creative ways to get rid of a body, but unfortunately, none of those options are available to me. And honestly, I can't take the stench much longer. Rigor mortis is setting in, the smell of death becoming stronger. I have to get him out of here before he starts decomposing.

One thing I'll give him credit for is moving out in the middle of nowhere. Other than the neighbor across the street, there's no one else for as far as I can see. I don't know if it's a man or woman occupying the house, but I need to get him buried before I find out. Hopefully, it's an elderly person that goes to bed early.

Grabbing a few fifty-five-gallon trash bags from the kitchen, I decided to cover his upper body with one, and his lower body with the other. As I kneel beside him, gripping the back of his neck to lift him up, I jerk away, his head thumping against the floor. I'm taken aback by his cool skin and stiff body.

I didn't think this through very well.

He's too big to drag him outside by myself.

And he's too stiff to fold his body into a bag.

Sitting back on my heels, I blow a stray hair out of my face, cursing Atlas's dead spirit for getting me into this mess.

It's well after midnight by the time I'm finished bagging his body.

After an hour of going back and forth, I went into the garage, looking for something. Anything to solve my problem. As luck would have it, I found a hacksaw on a tool bench. I debated whether my stomach was strong enough to do what needed to be done, but sheer determination pushed those worries aside. It also shoved past the ick of dragging his big ass into the bathtub.

It took a few hours to completely saw through his legs and arms. By the time I detached his torso, I was exhausted and cranky, my arms like jelly. But I fought through it, knowing I still had to remove his head.

Honestly, I wish I would've decapitated him first. The entire time I dismembered him, his milky eyes were trained on me. I tried to close his eyelids, but they kept snapping open, and eventually I gave up. I placed a dish towel over his eyes once I began sawing through his neck. It was brutal and messy but rather satisfying. I know I'll be sore tomorrow, but the pain will be worth it.

Afterwards, I stuffed all his pieces into the trash bags, and hauled them outside one by one, around to the back of the house.

Fuck my life.

I still have to dig a grave.

Heading back to the garage, I grab the shovel I saw earlier and get to work digging a hole behind the house. My arms ache as I stab the hard ground, sweat slicking my entire body, and I think I may pass out.

I've decided I'm not going to run, not now anyway. I'll take advantage of my death and use my new identity to begin a new life. From what I found with the search engine on Atlas's phone, I'm a couple of hours from the Asylum. No one knew I existed before going into that prison, and unless I run into Halstead at the one gas station in town, I don't believe anyone will recognize me.

"Hey." A male voice calls out behind me.

Whirling around, I raise the shovel behind me, ready to swing at the stranger's head.

His hands fly up in front of him. "Whoa there, wild cat."

"Who the fuck are you?" I snarl, already debating if I can handle cutting up another body tonight.

Absolutely not.

"Jaxson. I live across the street." He winks, his friendly demeanor confusing the hell out of me since it's very obvious I'm digging a fucking grave.

"Just you?"

He chuckles. "Yeah, just me. But I do have people who'll ask questions if I don't show up to work on Monday. So don't do to me whatever you did to that poor bastard."

I scoff. "He deserved worse than what he got."

Fuck.

I just outed myself.

Jaxson's gaze hardens. "I know."

My eyes widen. "*How* do *you* know?"

He stuffs his hands in his pockets, looking sheepish. "I came over when I heard the yelling. I'd seen you before when he occasionally opened the curtains. I wanted to make sure he wasn't hurting you."

Dropping the shovel, my ass hits the ground, my body running on fumes. "You couldn't stomach what he's done to me."

He inches closer, like he's approaching a rabid dog. Once he realizes I won't bite, he sits beside me, leaving a few feet between us. "What's your name, wild cat?"

I grin at the nickname. "Do you want my real name, or the one he gave me?"

He shuffles closer. "The real one."

"Olivia."

"What name did he give you?"

"Lilly."

He scrunches up his face. "No offense, but you're no *Lilly*."

A laugh bursts from my lips, and it feels good, yet foreign. He smiles, and it's like a punch to the gut. Jaxson is tall, built, and has a face any woman would be honored to sit on. He's a sexy fucking man, making Atlas seem like a steaming pile of dog shit.

His smile turns cocky as if he can sense my thoughts, and my cheeks burn with embarrassment. He stands abruptly, reaching for the discarded shovel beside me.

"What are you doing?" I ask, standing up, dusting off my ass.

"You're gorgeous, wild cat, but you look exhausted. I'm

going to dig this grave and throw him in it. After that, we'll get you cleaned up so you can get some rest."

My brows furrow. "Why?"

He grins. "It's the neighborly thing to do."

"Why aren't you freaking out or calling the cops?" I ask, waiting for the ball to drop.

He winks before slamming the shovel into the hard ground, his eyes softening as he glances up at me. "Let's just say I have a few skeletons in my back yard, too."

ACKNOWLEDGMENTS

Thank you to the Wellard Asylum Shared World for allowing me to collaborate in this series. I'm grateful for the opportunity to work with so many wonderful authors.

A huge thank you to my beta readers. Katelin and Amber, thank you for listening to all my ramblings and my ridiculous thought process. I'm thankful I have you two to keep me grounded when I'm overwhelmed or indecisive. I love you both. Kizzie, you're truly a gem to have on this journey. You're the ultimate hype girl for Indie Authors, and I'm grateful to have your love and support. Kenzie, you're an absolute doll, and your support of Indie Authors is a beautiful thing to witness.

Thank you to my ARC readers for always showing up and being amazing. You're the last line of defense before my books are released into the wild. I'm grateful for your feedback, and for catching any last minute oopsies before release day.

Finally, to my readers. I just love you. There's not much to say other than that. You take a chance on me, and that alone is a triumph for me. All of you crazy heathens take the time to read my books, and it still surprises me how many of you love them. You're the reason I keep writing. Your love and support means everything to me.

BOOKS BY THIS AUTHOR

His Good Girl

Formerly married to a cruel narcissist, I've been content in my solitary existence the past two years.

At least, that's what I tell myself.

Until I lock eyes with him.

He's gorgeous, confident, and covered in ink.

Suddenly, I don't want to be alone anymore.

It begins like a script for a spicy romance novel, a second chance at finding love.

But the past comes back with a vengeance, and ours collide in a way we never could've imagined.

Rage

All I've ever known is violence.

After being abused by the people closest to me, I despise being touched.

Many nights of my past were spent wishing for death.

The time came when I'd had enough.

I snapped, taking back my life while ending another.

Things took a turn for the better, but defending myself never changed.

The night a stranger put his hands on me in the park, my blade came out to play.

I wasn't counting on the gorgeous stranger witnessing my wrath.

I didn't expect him to watch me from the shadows every night after.

I want to hate him, but his dark eyes and deadly past have me intrigued.

No matter how much I push him away, or want to kill him, I don't.

His filthy words unravel me.

His touch sets me on fire.

As darkness collides, obsession turns into something deeper.

He knows my secrets.

He's earned my trust.

He owns my body.

Giving him my heart?

It may get us both killed...

Chaos

Life was normal until it wasn't.

My family was gone in the blink of an eye, and I ran.

The tough girl with a chip on her shoulder ran like a coward.

Ran straight into an existence full of guilt and despair, hiding for the past two years.

Other than my nine to five, I lock myself in my apartment, terrified he'll find me and kill me.

I'm alone.

I'm lost.

I'm waiting for it all to end.

By my hand or his.

An innocent question to the stranger next-door changes everything.

He pushes his way into my life, offering protection from a past he knows nothing about.

Or so I think.

A split-second decision changes my life in ways I never imagined.

Death brings life and it changes me forever.

Secrets are revealed and everything unravels.

I'm not alone like I thought.

I'm not as hidden as I hoped.

The man who ripped my life apart has only one obsession.

To see me dead.

Reaper

Trauma changes a person.

When I met the devil at eight years old, it changed the course of my life.

Lost and alone, anger controlled my every thought.

Happiness was out of reach until the day I found my calling.

At sixteen years old, they never saw me coming.

As an adult, I'm the Reaper they fear.

Seeking vengeance for all the victims who were silenced.

Darkness ruled my world until I laid eyes on her.

A sliver of light trickled into my life, and I would do anything to hold onto it.

I stole her heart.

I own her soul.

She's my wife.

The one person I'd give my life to protect at any cost.

She thinks she knows all my secrets.

The man she loves is a serial killer and she doesn't have a clue.

Or does she?

It seems she has a secret of her own.

When lies are exposed and the truth is revealed, our lives will change forever.

Devil

They call him Devil.

They say darkness follows him wherever he goes.

They say he's a dangerous man, a monster.

They made him seem like a demon from your nightmares.

They'll whisper about me.

They'll question my sanity.

They'll warn me away from him.

I'm the lost girl who fell in love with the devil.

We knew each other in another life.

Before the darkness consumed us completely.

He was the quiet boy who stared at me from across the room.

I was the sad girl, terrified to trust anyone.

One night changed it all.

Everything went up in smoke.

He disappeared, taking a part of me with him.

The silent teenager is long gone, but the ruthless man who's returned is the devil.

And he's brought the depths of hell with him to protect me.

Unholy Night

A blanket of snow covers the ground.

The world is silent under the moonlit sky.

All is calm, except for one thing.

Someone is watching me.

This Christmas Eve will be an Unholy Night to remember.

ABOUT THE AUTHOR

J. S. Cannon is a self-published Indie Author with a passion for writing dark romance with strong female characters and obsessive male leads. Her writing journey began with sweet and spicy novellas but evolved into a love of creating stories with morally gray characters and witty banter. Whether you're looking for a book with darker elements, or a tale with gore and torture, she offers something for every spicy reader.

J. S. Cannon lives with her husband, a Great Pyrenees, a Boxador, and a Snowshoe Siamese cat, all adding warmth, chaos, and laughter to her everyday life. She enjoys reading all genres of romance, her favorites being dark, fantasy, and horror. Reading and writing are her two favorite hobbies, as well as gaming and spending time with her family.

Printed in Dunstable, United Kingdom